Comfort Me with Spies

By Marc Lovell

COMFORT ME WITH SPIES
ETHEL AND THE NAKED SPY
THE SPY WHO FELL OFF THE BACK OF A BUS
THAT GREAT BIG TRENCHCOAT IN THE SKY
GOOD SPIES DON'T GROW ON TREES
THE SPY WHO BARKED IN THE NIGHT
THE SPY WHO GOT HIS FEET WET
THE ONE GOOD APPLE IN A BARREL OF SPIES
HOW GREEN WAS MY APPLE
APPLE TO THE CORE
APPLE SPY IN THE SKY
SPY ON THE RUN
THE SPY WITH HIS HEAD IN THE CLOUDS
THE SPY GAME
THE LAST SEANCE
HAND OVER MIND
SHADOWS AND DARK PLACES
AND THEY SAY YOU CAN'T BUY HAPPINESS
THE HOSTAGE GAME
A VOICE FROM THE LIVING
THE SECOND VANETTI AFFAIR
THE GUARDIAN SPECTRE
THE BLIND HYPNOTIST
DREAMERS IN A HAUNTED HOUSE
FOG SINISTER
AN ENQUIRY INTO THE EXISTENCE OF VAMPIRES
THE GHOST OF MEGAN
A PRESENCE IN THE HOUSE
THE IMITATION THIEVES

MARC LOVELL

Comfort Me with Spies

A CRIME CLUB BOOK
DOUBLEDAY
New York London Toronto Sydney Auckland

8/13

A CRIME CLUB BOOK
PUBLISHED BY DOUBLEDAY
a division of Bantam Doubleday Dell Publishing Group, Inc.
666 Fifth Avenue, New York, New York 10103

All of the characters in this book are fictitious,
and any resemblance to actual persons, living or
dead, is purely coincidental.

Library of Congress Cataloging-in-Publication Data

Lovell, Marc.
Comfort me with spies / Marc Lovell. — 1st ed.
p. cm.
"A Crime Club book."
I. Title.
PR6062.0853C6 1990
823'.914—dc20 89-28157
CIP

ISBN 0-385-26795-9

Printed in the United States of America
June 1990
First Edition

BG

Comfort Me with Spies

ONE

The man came charging at him with a scream. Apple gagged in shock. He didn't know or care which shattered him most, the scream loud enough and fiendish enough to dry his mouth, or the man's awesome appearance; he just gagged.

Mere seconds ago they had shaken hands, and the man, called Tiny Bomb, had even wished him the best of luck—this while wearing a smile on his cheery face. Now those same lips were twisted like a maniac's, and the face had the aspect of a savage's when he plunges the spear in.

Apple dodged aside.

Thundering past, Tiny Bomb hit the ropes and bounced off into a spin. His elegance and perfection, considering the size of the man, were almost as surprising as had been his change in personality.

Tiny Bomb stood well over six feet tall and weighed in the famineless region of two hundred and twenty pounds. Naked apart from trunks and soft-leather boots, muscles rippled under his glistening skin like too many mice in the breadbag.

He began to come forward in another sudden

change of mien: at a panther creep, as though suspicious of his opponent's reserve.

Warily Apple backed away. He was recovering his emotional balance. He managed to ignore that he was aiming to get behind the referee, just as he was taking no notice of the jeers coming from the crowded seats.

Someone catcalled, "Don't be so brash, Silver Flash!"

The audience responded to the poet with laughter. Several others tried their luck for fleeting celebrity and even the ring's third man chuckled, "Think of the cash, Flash."

All Apple was thinking of was the quickest and most painless way of losing, without being too obvious about it.

Arms raised on high like a gorilla annoyed, Tiny Bomb stalked after his opponent with evil in every feature. He growled and sprang forward.

This time Apple was too slow in doing a sideways dodge. His shoulder and Tiny Bomb's collided, the sound like a dead pig being dropped on marble.

Apple was hurled away.

The crowd roared as he staggered around the ring in a large circle, speed enabling him both to keep on his feet and to avoid Tiny Bomb's grabbing hands. The eighteen thousand spectators of Empress Hall coasted before his eyes like a rotating mural of happy peasants.

Apple finished up backed into a corner. Tiny Bomb was posed in the middle of the ring, arms folded high. He appeared to be as confident as if he were matched against a midget.

Apple, alias Appleton Porter, alias Silver Flash, was six feet seven inches tall. His frame had merely a sufficiency of flesh, however, not an excess. Compared to the Bomb, he was one of those matchstick figures that live in diagrams.

Nevertheless, Apple did fairly well with his impersonation of a professional wrestler in the silver boots, silver trunks and silver hood. The last was especially useful. Kept tight by means of a zip at the back, showing mouth, nose, eyes and ears, and made of an open-knit material that allowed the entry of cooling air, the hood hid those features which Apple would have been as happy to hide forever as he would to lose half a foot off his height.

Neat sandy hair, eyes of an innocent green, freckle-dotted pale skin that cruelly showed every blush, regular features with no signs of damage—people would have asked, "Can this be a pro who has spent a decade pounding canvas?"

There were some who would have said, furthermore, those who might happen to see press or television coverage of events, "Why, that's good old Appleton Porter of the United Kingdom Philological Institute. He couldn't wrestle his way out of a damp shirt." It was an outside possibility that had to be considered. Thus the dual-purpose hood.

Tiny Bomb came forward at a saunter, hands mashing each other heavily. Even through the crowd's roar, the cracking of knuckles could be heard, or so Apple believed. It spurred him into making a surprise move.

Holding on to the top ropes of his corner, he swung up both legs. His boots caught his opponent flat on the chest. According to theory he ought to have gone over backwards; instead, he simply halted and then took one step in reverse.

After whimpering a curse, Apple tried to escape

from the corner. Although he was able to slip under Tiny Bomb's arm, which resembled the branch of a tree, he didn't get far. Two large hands grabbed hold of him, one under the knee and one above the elbow.

Apple found himself rising off the canvas. Next, released from the grip, he was flying through space. Even while scared, he was telling himself knowledgeably, That's the Hamilton Hurl.

In descending, Apple landed well: hands first, shoulders next, hip last, the whole turned into a roll. He ended lying prone with his upper body under the bottom rope and out on the apron. People in the front rows welcomed him with jeers and cheers. One man threw a handful of popcorn.

As one piece bounced off his nose, Apple wondered if he could get away with quitting right now, perhaps with the claim of having a dislocated joint. Sadly he was forced to admit that it was too soon yet.

He felt his ankles grabbed. After being dragged into the ring's centre, he had his legs twisted by the Bomb. His body crashed painfully from front to back and to front again. Then he was released so he could go on crashing.

He came to a halt sprawled on the bottom rope, once more gazing over the near seating.

One person caused his weary attention to snap alert, his aching body to be passingly forgotten, his self-sympathy to take a break. That person, sitting on the front row, was a distinctive blonde.

In her mid-thirties, she had a mass of curly hair, a face whose beauty came as a surprise after the accompanying glitz, jewellery and a tight whore-red dress with a hem as high as its neckline was low.

Observing that Agnes de Grace wore panties to

match her dress, Apple smiled a tentative greeting. The cool blonde crossed her sumptuous thighs and brought into place a view-blocking purse.

Apple straightened his head.

At which point his ankles were grabbed again. Retaliating toughly, he told himself, but in reality being taken by an unacknowledged schoolboy urge to show off, he did a vicious knee-jerk to break the grip.

This worked so well, he saw on twisting around, that Tiny Bomb was thrown off balance. Apple leapt to his feet and lunged forward, a Watson Crunch in mind. Too late he saw the trap. Tiny Bomb had been acting. He met the lunge with a forearm smash to the neck.

That was Apple's first burst of pain. The next was when he crashed down on his back. The third came as Tiny Bomb dropped flat across his chest to pin him for a count of three.

Making feeble attempts to get free, Apple wondered dazedly, rhetorically, how he came to be here in the first place.

For a second or two, as the small figure materialised beside him and kept pace with his stride, Apple thought he was about to have the bite put on him.

He perked with interest. Now he would have to decide on his response. Should he give alms so as to enjoy feeling sympathetic, decent, generous, or should he decline in order to get a kick out of being a deadbeat?

"If you could slow down, mate," the figure said in uncompromising Cockney.

Apple stopped. Albert did the same. Looking up with an exaggerated back-tilt of his head, he murmured, "Bit of cloud over the summit today." It was one of his standards.

Apple had become a broth of clashing emotions. There was the disappointment of being cheated out of his decision. There was his dislike of the cretinesque Albert. There was embarrassment for the little man on account of his gross sense of humour. There was discomfort from admitting he would like to see him hospitalised, preferably with something people wouldn't talk about. There was a muffled fury in knowing that someone half his size and twice his age could tie him in knots.

Most of all, by far the strongest of all, there was a throb of excitement.

Apple allowed the last its rightful position and pushed all others back to where they belonged, the realm of the inconsequential.

He said, "Nice to see you again, Albert."

The little man looked passingly depressed. Grey-haired and mongrel-faced, he wore his defeated blue boilersuit with a particular lack of panache, as if he believed such garments were the very essence of style and was determined to show how blasé he could be about it all.

"Looking in the pink, as usual," Apple said loudly.

Albert accused, "You wasn't at the lingo works." He meant the august United Kingdom Philological Institute.

"Sore throat."

"You wasn't in your attic." He meant the ample apartment in Harlequin Mansions, Bloomsbury.

"Out shopping," Apple said. By way of proof he lifted and rattled a paper bag.

"I soon figured that out," Albert said. "And I came

here and found you." He indicated Goudge Street's commercial clamour, not without a hint of bored ownership, as though he had discovered it first.

"You knew I shopped here?"

"Course."

Lowering his bag after a final rattle, Apple said, "That's pretty smart of you." He winced inside at the crudeness of his flattery.

Albert's answer was to shake his head. "Sore throat, eh? Bit awkward, that."

Even while seeing through this pathetic bid for extra power, even while knowing that nothing would be changed if he had no throat at all, Apple said a fast, "It's better. I took antibiotics and it cleared up like magic." He nodded anxiously. "Pure magic."

Doubtfully: "You sure?"

"Positive."

"Say Mary Had a Little Lamb, and all the rest of it. Let's hear how you sound."

There were limits beyond which Apple refused to go in being a toady, and one of these was reciting like a good little fellow.

Coldly, he said, "No, thank you."

"Why not?"

"I don't remember the words."

"You could say 'em after me."

Seized with bravery, Apple said, "I have to be running along." He moved forward. "See you around, Albert." He walked on.

"Sure. See you."

For a terrible, thrilling moment Apple thought the older man was going to let him go. But, of course, whether Albert liked it or not he had to complete his errand; he was no less an underling than Apple himself.

Drably, Albert called out, "Follow me."

Swinging around, seeing the little man walking off in the other direction, Apple set out in pursuit. His knees had a thrum of relief. His excitement thrived. He didn't mind the unromantic presence of his paper bag.

Resisting the desire to feel sorry for Albert, or be irked that he didn't at least have the manners to pretend to check whether he was being followed, Apple contented himself with staying far enough back to serve his several purposes.

He didn't want anyone to get the idea he was associated with his Control's scruffy courier/valet/bodyguard; he didn't want to be made to look taller by comparison; he didn't want to miss this opportunity of doing some tailing.

Apple wasn't exactly overworked in his connexion with the department of British Intelligence known as Upstairs. In the past decade he had been sent out into the field as an operative so seldom that it would average out almost to an annual event. It was no help to his career that success on these occasions had had the frequency of Leap Year.

In Apple's secret life his major contribution was via language. In the cant of espionage, he was a speakfreak. So many foreign tongues did he own that, in order not to seem a show-off or a liar to enquirers, he usually gave the number as a mere eight.

With his legitimate job as a senior official at the Philological Institute, Apple was able to work overtly as an interpreter at international meetings, political and military, where he served as an ear for whatever was in the air; covertly he worked as a translator of documents which went as high as Top Very Most Secret, which meant fairly close to the head of the classified list.

Appleton Porter scored a solid 10 in Security Clearance. In other areas he was not so golden. During his training days he had scored only 6's in Acting Ability and Lying Skill, poor 5's in Resistance to Pain and Tolerance for Alcohol.

There were further reasons why his services as a spy were rarely required, apart from the obvious drawback of his height, which made blending with the crowd a considerable project. He had four habits or conditions which were condemned in his dossier as Unfortunate.

One, he fell in love frequently, easily, and with the thoroughness of a pimple-clad youth.

Two, he collected snippets of information which could only be described as useless, such as the licence number of the taxi that knocked down and killed the author of *Gone With the Wind* in Atlanta, Georgia. This habit was thought to make for absent-mindedness, at the least.

Three, he was inclined to feel sympathetic toward other people, even if said other people happened to be on the opposite side in the spy game.

Four, he was a blusher. Not one of your average sensitive types who pink up at the outrageous, but a true sufferer who went crimson at absurdities such as not being able to remember authors' names.

In respect of active duty, Apple secretly doubted if he would ever be anything other than a member of the brigade of faceless ones, those people who were on call to Upstairs for the occasional job because of some peculiarity—the ability to tightrope walk, scream a C above high C, hear over a long distance, or send Morse while listening to music and holding a conversation and absorbing a film.

Apple, however, had not given up hope. And meanwhile he kept in practice by various ploys, one being to tail undersized men in boilersuits.

The car was two streets away.

As directed, Apple got into the rear behind the driver, a man as nondescript as the vehicle itself. Albert got in the front. He lifted a telephone receiver off the dashboard, mumbled into it, listened a moment and then passed the instrument back, mouthing in respectful silence, "God."

Into the receiver Apple said, "Good day, sir."

The plain brown voice of Angus Watkin answered. "You have been found, Porter."

"Yes, sir. Sorry about causing problems. I wasn't expecting an emergency."

Slowly, softly, Watkin said, "He wasn't expecting an emergency."

"Well. You know."

"Never mind, Porter. This isn't one in any case. We have a week."

Apple asked, "A week in which to do what, sir?"

Typically, his Control ignored him, asking back, "How well do you wrestle?"

"Very well, sir. I'm good at it."

"I thought so. Not that it matters. You will be taught the basics so that you'll be able to pretend, at any rate long enough to suffice."

"Yes, sir," Apple said crisply. "Does this mean . . ."

"That will be all for now, Porter," Angus Watkin said. "Go home and pack a suitcase." The line died.

• • •

Waving the two men forward, the referee chanted, "First fall to Tiny Bomb. Two falls to go."

All he needed to do, Apple mused as he sank into the crouch of a predator, was let himself get pinned again as soon as possible, and it would be all over. But he ought to make a good showing.

With the crowd roaring, as though encouraging slavering dogs, Apple and Tiny Bomb circled one another in an atavistic dance. The latter wore confidence like a niftily-stolen hat.

Without moving his head, Apple glanced aside and down. Agnes de Grace was watching intently, leaning forward, the tip of her tongue peeping out in a way that made Apple think, disappointingly, not of the erotic but of a child watching illicitly through the bannister rails. He hoped he wasn't going to get any stupid, romantic notions about the lady.

Tiny Bomb's charge caught him full on. He went careening backwards. After sloughing into the ropes, he catapulted back wildly, arms waving like a gale-maddened windmill, head down in self-protection.

The head made a solid contact with the chin of Tiny Bomb. The gasp of pain he gave was louder than Apple's, his rebound from the collision greater, his fall to the canvas more decisive.

Apple jumped up immediately. With equal immediacy he realised his mistake: he should have stayed down. He sighed; once again he had been betrayed by having a body whose reflexes were too fast for his mind. Blame thus disposed of, and not unflatteringly, he wondered if he could get away with collapsing back to the canvas.

Apple let go of this idea on noting that his opponent

was still down there. Spread-eagled on his back, eyes closed, Tiny Bomb lay without a hint of movement anywhere except in his chest. The referee was shouting in his ear.

Next moment, it seemed, the ring was busy with people. Tiny Bomb was being helped to his feet, the referee was lifting Apple's arm and the crowd was roaring. Trumpets began to sound a clarion and cameras flashed.

Apple felt as though he were growing. The sensation ought to have been anathema to him, but was not. It wasn't even slightly unpleasant. It was wonderful. For the first time in his life, he had gained the limelight.

Apple didn't care that he was supposed to have lost the match, that some in the crowd were claiming a foul, that the trumpet clarion kept slurring as the tape slipped, or that his win was accidental. He was a conquering hero.

Freed by the referee, Apple stalked around beside the ropes, both arms raised, his critical faculties brutally supressed. His eyes were agleam, his grin was wide.

He became aware of what he had given little mind to before: the television cameras. There were four, each set midway back in the seating. Apple gave them the benefit of himself in profile and full frontal.

He went on doing this, and circling the ring blowing kisses, clasping his hands on high and making a pair of V's for victory signs, even when the crowd was settling. The trumpet tape had been switched off and the ring had emptied of everyone except the referee. Apple suspected himself of being obnoxious, if not disgusting.

"Fight's over and done, Silver Flash," the referee told him. "You can go now."

In the name of good manners Apple made one final tour of the ring before getting through the ropes. Jumping down, he graciously allowed a handler to put his silver cape around him before he set off up the aisle. He waved to either side. He forgave the television cameras for being focussed elsewhere.

Not until he was in the shower did Apple return from the glory of it all. Even so, he refused to be depressed because he had failed to lose, or had forgotten to note how Agnes de Grace was taking his victory. What would be would be. The game was only beginning.

Modestly wrapped in a towel, Apple came out of the showers into a long changing room where all fittings were dark blue, just as in the other changing room they were all red. This served to remind wrestlers, not noted for the keenness of their minds, to which corner of the ring they belonged.

The colour scheme reminded Apple first of the convenience of segregation (opponents not having to go through the hypocrisies of behaving decently toward one another). Secondly, he was reminded that he had just interfered with the career of a wrestler who, after all, did have to make a living and take care of his responsibilities.

Swiftly, before he could start worrying—worrying he would not enjoy, it being real rather than contrived —Apple strode along to the locker he had been allocated and started to dress.

The room held a dozen men. They were lounging, sitting, changing. The last would be having bouts this afternoon. All, in turn, either called across their congratulations to Apple or came with a handshake. That the call and handshake were automatic, perfunctory, Apple accepted as part of a business wherein bouts were almost as frequent as Friday.

So here he was, Apple thought comfortably as he sat on the bench to tie shoelaces. Here he was at work in Empire, Ontario. He had arrived and survived. He was easing into a caper that sometime might come under the heading of That Peculiar Little Affair in Canada.

In bright moments Apple allowed himself to peek at his secret conviction that one day, perhaps, far in the future, maybe, when he was quite old, possibly, a book would be written about the exploits of Appleton Russell Porter, spy.

During that initial encounter in the ring, Apple dreamily mused the piece might run, *agent Porter made brilliant use of the ropes, in a ploy he had invented himself to put his opponent out of action, for he had shrewdly concluded that to fall at the first fence, as it were, would tend to rouse . . .*

"Congrats, S.F."

Snapping alert, Apple stood up to take the proffered hand. His alertness went beyond the social when he recognised the man, who was only two inches shorter than himself. He went under the professional name of Bull Massive.

"Thank you," Apple said. "And may I say, Mr. Massive, it's a treat to meet one of the top men in the business."

"Thanks. But call me B.M., mm?"

"With pleasure."

Wearing white slacks, bright green blazer and purple open-neck shirt, the wrestler measured about a yard across the shoulders and two around the waist. His head was shaved bald. His face was that of almost any big thirty-year-old who had been thumped regularly over a long period. Both ears were of the type called cauliflower, a misnomer, for they more closely resembled boiled figs.

"Perhaps I should've said *the* top man," Apple amended. "You've even beaten Japan's finest wrestler, I know."

"Yeah, that's right. In Kyoto."

"In January of last year."

The bald man grinned. "Hey, right on, S.F."

Apple said, "Maybe we could get together sometime. I'd like to hear about that."

"Give me a call and we'll see. I'm staying at the Puck Motel."

"So'm I."

A minute later, the wrestler having lumbered away, Apple was finishing his lace-tying and feeling grateful for all he had been forced to absorb at Damian House.

The country mansion, surrounded by parklike acreage, was believed by locals to be a place of rest and recuperation for armed forces personnel. In reality one of the Secret Service's training centres, it was unguarded save for hidden video cameras at the gate and a surround of alarm trip-wire disguised as the barbed variety, suitably drooping and rusted.

Apple was no stranger to Damian House. Here he had done his early training, a decade ago, when he had believed he was about to embark on a career romantic, dangerous and exciting. He still sometimes believed it was waiting for him right around the corner.

These times happened whenever he returned to

Damian House for refreshers or special courses, and was infected by memories of his youthful innocence.

Jacking his spirits higher on this visit was the respect shown him by a group of initiates. To these he represented himself via word or wink or sigh as the embattled pro, newly returned from a hellish mission abroad and already being primed for yet another. His embarrassment at his crassness and posing he managed to keep hidden from himself.

One apprentice spy in particular, named Jill, was so impressed by Apple's last exploit—which he told her of in the strictest confidence during their first walk in the woods, and which he had stolen from Eric Ambler—that on their third nightly trip outdoors they spent more time lying down than walking. Thereafter, weather chill, it was a matter of "your room or mine."

Busy with his posturing and romancing, plus drink-buying for those who could give him away if they were so inclined, Apple vaguely resented the attentions of his mentors.

He had three. One taught him the basics of all-in wrestling, one pure wrestling's history; a third talked to him about Bull Massive, Agnes de Grace and Samuel Glacier. The first mentor he saw most.

Apple spent hours every day in the basement gym bouncing around the ring with Joe, who was short, fat and ugly. He coached his tired pupil from *A* to *Z*, from the Anaconda to Zola's Charge. Not once did he mention that he had been a star on the pro circuit, which Apple thought unfair of him since he knew of Apple's tall tales.

"Listen," Joe said on one of their first sessions, after trying to get Apple to make realistic grunts and moans. "Forget Cornish, Cumberland, Greco-Roman and all the rest of 'em. They're legit and respectable and boring. This is a different kettle of fish altogether."

Apple asked, "But is it wrestling?"

"Course it is."

"Is it sport?"

"It has no governing bodies, if that's what you mean. There's very few rules and regulations. There's no limits on age or size: a flyweight can fight a heavyweight, if he wants, if he has no better sense."

"Corruption?"

"There's practically none of that involved because, while a bout hasn't necessarily been fixed, it will often be won by the wrestler who lost against this same opponent when they were last matched together. Fair's fair, after all."

Apple said, "A sport it isn't, then."

"Listen," Joe said, patient. "You must've seen a bullfight at some time or another."

"What's the connexion?"

"Pro grappling is a more polite form of that, *la corrida,* with the death and stigma removed. You could take the kiddies to see wrestling. You could take anyone. Your mum. In fact, it appeals especially to middle-aged women."

"Why? Is it what they've always wanted to do to the men in their lives?"

"That's certainly a part of it. In any case, it's a form of violence they're not ashamed of being seen lapping up, and not uniquely—there's dozens of others around them."

Apple stated, "Comradeship."

"That's another part of it, yes. And along with the company we've got the suggestion of sport, the laughter and entertainment, the bounding good health of the combatants, the spectacle and colour, the show-biz ambience, the excitement, and, most of all, we have the therapeutic angle."

"Sado-masochistic release?"

"Yes," Joe said. "So, we have all those together and they're wrapped inside the simple, obvious fact that the guy who's taken the biggest battering usually gets up off the floor toward the end of the bout, and wins. The worm turns."

"Therefore we also have someone to pull for," Apple said. "A hero."

"And the louder we shout in pulling, the better for us. The primal scream syndrome. Professional wrestling is healthier to watch than anything I know of."

"Sounds it."

Joe asked, "Anything else you want to know before we get back to grunts?"

"Yes. Why am I being taught all this?"

"No idea. But I'll ask around. Someone's sure to have the info. This bloody place is full of finks and spies."

Apple still didn't know any more about the mission when, week concluded, it was time to say good-bye to Jill and hello to Angus Watkin.

Empire, Ontario, population 40,000, home of the Empire Builders, one of Canada's best ice-hockey teams, whose venue, Empress Hall, could be converted to other uses from basketball to wrestling. Local industries: tourism, manufacture of ice-skates, fruit-canning.

Apple quoted facts to himself like a sleeping museum guide as he came out of the stadium's stage door into Indian summer warmth. This was to prove to himself that he was unconcerned that the twenty or so people waiting in the alley, some of them attractive young women, were paying him not the slightest heed. Worse, several waiters even put their autograph books behind their backs.

Fans left behind, Apple walked along the service lane and went back to enjoying the freedom of being in shirt and jeans. To a man accustomed to wearing ultra-conservative clothes in public, the ensemble was as refreshing as shorts to a sheik.

Apple came out onto the town's broad, main thoroughfare, Emperor Avenue. Under the stadium's marquee a straggle of people fed to the box office; buyers of tickets for future sessions. Neither they nor the passers-by gave unusual attention to Apple; he wasn't the only tall specimen in town this week.

Apple went through glass doors. From the girl behind a popcorn machine he learned that Samuel Glacier had gone to his hotel; the Royal, she thought.

"I'm staying at the Puck myself," Apple said. Since the girl didn't tell him that meant he must be one of the wrestlers, he was about to tell her he was one of the wrestlers when she said, with a sniff:

"They say the place is full of wrestlers."

"Really?"

"None of the real stars, of course. Except for Bull Massive. He always stays there. Popcorn?"

"I hate it."

"That's how I feel about the grunt and groan boys. But Bull Massive, he's different."

"Good-bye."

After pausing at the doors to call back that he was only kidding, popcorn was okay, Apple left. He walked to where he had parked his rented Ford. In late sunshine he drove slowly along Emperor. Where the stores faded began motels and other fringe endeavours.

Apple eased to a stop at a traffic light on red. The car that drew up beside him, a beach buggy which he knew and coveted, was driven by a man in his twenties, with a round face and heavy tan, fair hair under a yachting cap, T-shirt and dungarees. He wore a whimsical expression.

Apple asked, "Are you following me, Chuck?"

In a Canadian accent, the man asked back, "Would I do that?"

"Don't look now, but your training's showing: always answer direct questions with questions."

"No comment."

"Ditto."

The man known as Chuck said, "I hear you won your bout."

"It was an accident."

"It's not *my* problem."

The traffic light changing, Apple shot away. His speed had nothing to do with his local Intelligence contact; it was because he disliked being honked at, for the shortest time lapse measurable, he knew, was that between a light turning green and the driver behind you honking.

When Apple slowed to legal, the beach buggy drew alongside. Chuck said, "There's no need to get mad."

"I'm not," Apple said, adding, "Driving on the wrong side of the road in North America makes me nervous." As before, he, like the other man, stayed facing front while talking.

"Know what you mean. Same with me in Britain.

But what makes me more nervous is seeing all those policemen around with their pointed heads."

"Okay, okay."

"And I honestly wasn't following you, One," Chuck said. "I'll send you some anti-paranoia pills."

"Just so long as you send me what I need when I need it, if I do happen to need anything, which isn't all that likely, when you consider . . ." Having lost contact with his syntax, Apple waved a hand.

"And farewell to you too, Silver Flash," Chuck said. He zoomed ahead.

Disgruntled, Apple decided he no longer liked the beach buggy with all its flash. It wasn't that in liking it he had felt disloyal to Ethel, his retired London taxicab back home. The vehicle was just plain ugly.

Apple became more disgruntled, suspecting himself of being unfair, as well as juvenile and fatuous. This he covered by pretending to be annoyed at not having thought at the time what he thought of now, a crack to counter that one about bobbies' helmets. Chuck, of the Royal Canadian Mounted Police, wouldn't have taken kindly to a slur on their cowboy hats.

Except, Apple remembered, all of the RCMP officers he had seen since arriving in Canada had worn uniform caps. So holding back the crack had been a smart move.

Cheered, Apple drove on.

In a minute the Puck Motel appeared. Red brick, two stories high, it was shaped like a horseshoe around a swimming pool. In common with all the other motels hereabouts this week, it had its No Vacancy neon buzzing.

For the free feel of it, Apple drove in, circled the

pool, steered out and continued along the highway, which was beginning to thin out.

Outside a tavern, Apple saw what he had vaguely been seeking: a powder-blue Rolls-Royce convertible. Its white top was down, its anti-thief device in the back, tongue lolling.

Apple turned onto the forecourt. He parked and locked up. With a wink for Samuel Glacier's German Shepherd, which sized him up wistfully, he went to the tavern and into its dusky atmosphere.

There were loungers at the bar, players at a shuffleboard, five men and a pack of cards at a round table, and an old Roy Rogers episode on television (the wrestling was blacked out within a radius of one hundred miles).

Apple had the scene assessed before he got served at the bar with his ginger ale. Through a mirror he observed the man at the table who was being bank in blackjack.

Samuel Glacier had authority. It showed in his posture, in the solemnity of his lean, handsome face, in his flat tombstone-grey hair, in the way he had of dealing cards with an element of contempt, as if he owed them money. At forty-odd, he had the contained energy of a stripling and the manner of a sage. His conservative suit could have taken you anywhere.

This was Apple's third sighting of Samuel Glacier. And, as before, it looked as though he was going to be frustrated in his attempt to make contact beyond an hello. Glacier always seemed to be with company. He wasn't the type to take kindly to an interruption, certainly not while he was playing cards.

Apple sipped his drink, kept half an eye out for Trigger, reminded himself not to forget to send a postcard to his dog, Monico, and listened casually to the card players' talk between hands, which were curt and businesslike, a contrast to the talk's bright flow.

Time passed.

Apple was considering some outrageous attention-getter, such as loudly ordering champagne with chocolate milk, when Samuel Glacier, raking in bills, made a reference to the game of golf he would be having tomorrow morning at eleven.

That would do nicely, thank you very much, Apple thought. He left the tavern quietly, exchanging twilight and air-conditioning for sunshine and heat.

The North London pub was warm and bright after the morning's chilly gloom. Crossing the lounge, Apple felt benevolent toward his Control, whom he could see waiting at a table for two, and who, he mused, wasn't such a bad old stick.

Apple coughed to distract himself from that musing, which he disowned. If there was one thing Apple couldn't stand, it was hypocrisy. He tried to be forgiving, but if the hypocrisy were his own, he tended not so much to forgive as to forget.

He halted by the table. Standing not quite at attention, he said, "Good morning, sir." He noted the whiskey and his own favourite drink, sherry on the rocks. His Control knew his every idiosyncracy, which was tiresome for Apple as it denied him the right to feel enigmatic.

"Do sit down, Porter," Angus Watkin said in his spiritless voice. "Good morning."

This spy-master looked as mysterious as an open-face sandwich, as intriguing as rain. Medium was the word: size, shape, colouring, age, clothes, features. He appeared to have a talent for mediocrity. He was that man who, when he says, "Well," no one waits for the rest of it.

"Before you catch your plane later today," Watkin said, "you will be given your papers. You are Edward Parker of Manchester. The cover, which nobody is going to check, is simply to prevent a connexion with non-wrestling Appleton Porter."

"Yes, sir," Apple said. "And do I have a number-name in the operation?"

"You do. It's One."

"Thank you, sir."

"There being nobody else in the mission," Angus Watkin said, "it could hardly be other than that."

Pretending not to hear, a trick he had learned from Watkin himself, Apple asked, "And to what part of the world, sir, is the plane headed?"

"The Dominion of Canada. Your final destination is Empire, Ontario, where within days begins a tournament, which they're calling the Festival, to find the world's best wrestler, of the catch-as-catch-can species."

"The best in the world?"

"North American hyperbole," Angus Watkin said with a faint suggestion of happiness. He wasn't overly fond of the Mayflowers.

"Yes, sir," Apple murmured absently, relishing the thought of his Canadian trip.

"As far as professional wrestling is concerned, anyone can call himself champion, and most wrestlers do at some time or another. I'm not boring you, am I, Porter?"

Apple radiated alertness. "No, sir. I'm fascinated."

"In Empire, the competitors will be mostly from North America. The one who doesn't get eliminated will be crowned champion and receive a hefty check. Participants will also receive appearance money from TV, I understand."

"But these wrestlers are truly the best in the business?"

"Bone-crushers all, yes," Angus Watkin said. He sipped his drink while making a faint humming sound. "But a man who's had a week of training should come to little harm."

"True," Apple said like a negative.

"The whole venture is the dreamchild of one of your three marks, Samuel Glacier. He is the promoter, though he will be involved hardly at all in actual mechanics. Hirelings will do that. You know about Mr. Glacier."

"Professional gambler. Poker player of the first rank. Won a quarter million dollars at that game in Las Vegas a couple of years ago. A widower. Fan of golf, wrestling, horse racing, fine wines, beautiful—"

"Thank you, Porter."

"There's a lot more."

"Thank you all the same," Watkin said. "Don't forget your peculiar drink."

Apple obeyed like a conditioned dog. After gulping, he was furtive about wiping the dribble off his chin.

His Control said, "Samuel Glacier seems to be promoting this Festival on a whim. I doubt if he stands to make all that much money out of it. He has plenty of financial muscle, in any case."

"So he's not a sick gambler."

"He has no hidden yearning to lose, no."

"He's one of my marks, sir," Apple said. "The others must be Agnes de Grace and Bull Massive."

"Must you rush ahead, Porter?"

"Sorry, sir."

"Perhaps you have another engagement."

"Oh no, sir."

"I ought to remind you, by the by," Angus Watkin said, "of the rules against fraternising in the service with members of the opposite sex."

So much for finks and spies, Apple mused. He said, "Thank you, sir."

"And Miss de Grace? Briefly."

"Big Hollywood star ten years ago. Awful actress but an outstandingly attractive woman. She gave up movies to marry her fourth millionaire, who died three years ago. Fan of clothes, diamonds, new diets, pro wrestling, wild animals."

"Has she gone back to films, Porter?"

"No, sir. Too much competition from younger beauties, who, nowadays, can also act."

"Money?"

"Loaded as infallible dice," Apple said, quoting one of his Damian House mentors. "Her lifestyle is quietly lavish."

Angus Watkin had a drink of his Scotch. Apple followed, this time at such a turgid pace that he made no dribbles, just a loud noise when he swallowed.

"And Bull Massive?"

"Wife and five children. Been in wrestling since he was twenty. Has a vast number of fans and is well respected both in and out of the ring."

"You needn't go on," Angus Watkin said. "Respect, that's the operative word. Your three marks are respected. Tell me, what else do they have in common?"

"Well, sir, they're all Canadian. They're all into wrestling in one way or another. They're all financially comfortable. And they're all celebrities."

"*Popular* celebrities, Porter."

"Quite, sir."

"Fine," Angus Watkin said. "But the most important common factor is that they are all great supporters of a gentleman called Sid Street. You may have heard of him."

"No, sir," Apple said, cheerful about telling the truth, for he knew how dearly his chief loved being able to inform.

"He is an anarchist. From Montreal, French-Canadian, he preaches a free Quebec, civil disobedience, non-payment of federal taxes and lots of other aggravations. These are not so terrible in themselves, but people have died in following his beliefs, especially as regards an independent state of Quebec."

"In short, he's bad news."

Deafly, Watkin said, "Therefore, Porter, Ottawa is quite correct in wanting to neutralise Sid Street. The reason we are being invited to oblige, in return for a like favour, is, I hope, obvious."

"So Ottawa can keep its hands clean."

"Right. And the way to neutralise the gentleman is by stripping him of moral support, particularly in relation to your three marks. You follow?"

Apple said, "Yes, sir. Joe Public says these three people are terrific, and if they admire and support Sid Street he must have a lot going for him."

Angus Watkin nodded. "In a nutshell."

"So my job on this mission is to get the marks to withdraw their support for Street."

"No, Porter."

"Oh."

"That, naturally, has already been tried."

"Thought it might have," Apple lied.

Angus Watkin said, "What you have to do is discredit Agnes de Grace, Bull Massive and Samuel Glacier, who will all be in Empire next week."

"Discredit, sir?"

"You have to let the public see that the Trio, as we'll name them, are at fault in some way—taste, morals, judgment, what have you. So much at fault that anyone they admire must be equally flawed."

"Of course."

"Glad you agree, Porter. Makes all the difference."

Apple leaned forward to ask, "What, sir, are the Trio's vices, secret or otherwise?"

"Vices?" Angus Watkin said airily. "As far as I am aware, Porter, they don't have any. They seem to be rather straight, decent people."

Leaning back: "Ah."

"It's what you make them appear to be that counts, Porter, not what they are. And the time is ripe because Sid Street is out of the country at present."

With his chief talking on about the anarchist's travels, Apple worked at absorbing the fact that he was expected to destroy the reputations of three people who were acknowledged to be decent even by a master of cynicism such as Angus Watkin.

Apple was stunned.

When he tuned in fully again to his Control it was to hear about Silver Flash. That done, Watkin said, "Your presence in Empire as a wrestler is, naturally, simply to give you an in with the Trio. You will contrive to lose the first bout, and thereafter keep Silver Flash very much on the sidelines. The last thing you need is a high profile."

"Leave it to me, sir," Apple said.

TWO

Fluke or Foul? asked the minor headline. It was in the sports section of Empire's evening newspaper, the *Sentinel.* The story's gist was whether or not Silver Flash had deliberately butted Tiny Bomb, who had lost the match by default, being unable to continue.

There was no verdict, Apple was pleased to note, when he could stop looking proudly at the accompanying photograph of himself long enough to read the story closely. That the butt had been accidental, as he knew, he pretended not to know. Apple liked to believe that lurking in him somewhere was a comforting measure of evil.

He had bought the newspaper to read with his early dinner in the motel's coffee shop: small steak and salad. He would be wrestling again at ten. The piece on Silver Flash had come as a surprise dessert.

Profiles, low or otherwise, Apple had declined to consider, nor did he dwell on his actions during the hour he had strolled to and around town with the *Sentinel* under one arm, folded so the photograph was prominent; he was too busy considering angles in respect of the Trio, he had assured himself.

Now, realising he was sick of lugging the newspaper

around (no one had asked who that man was in the photo), Apple made use of a litter bin.

Minutes later, in the sporting goods store, open late this week like everything else, he told the girl, "I'm not Silver Flash, by the way, if that's what you were thinking." He had seen the danger of being recognized, if all worked out well.

The girl asked, "Who's Silver Flash?"

"Famous wrestler."

"They're a bunch of morons, you ask me. What make of golf ball did you want, sir?"

Leaving, Apple strolled along toward the Puck. As he tossed his golf ball from hand to hand he was reminded of the pros and cons he had gone through over the mission's aim. In the interim he became satisfied with his conclusion: if the three marks were truly decent they would fail to fall for whatever he cooked up.

Or something like that, Apple mused, more confident about that measure of evil's existence.

His next stop was at a street telephone box. For the third time since his arrival in Empire, Apple dialled Agnes de Grace's number. It belonged to a large house beyond the city limits rented by the actress for the Festival's duration.

A female voice answered. Mainly through the nose it said Madame was not at home, unfortunately. "Would you care to leave your name, sir?"

"No, thank you. I'm just a secret admirer. You might tell her that. Bye."

Strolling on in the dusk, nerves settling from their usual fight with his claustrophobia, even though he had kept the telephone box's door ajar, Apple felt as though he were doing fine, if not exactly making progress. Since he hadn't known what he was going to say to the woman with the elegant name, it was good that she hadn't been available.

When, on the motel's court, Apple was passing the swimming pool, prettily lit, a man detached himself from its furniture and came to make an interception. He was tall, thin, nervous, bespectacled, balding, glaring, pale, young, overdressed, pimply, buck-toothed, English.

The last established itself when he said, "You wouldn't happen to be Silver Flash, would you? They won't give me any information at the desk."

Apple said, "Er . . ."

"Only I'm a follower of wrestling—John Bark's the name—and I came over from Britain for the Festival. I can't imagine who this Englishman called Silver Flash is. Personally, I've never heard of him."

"I tink him famous," Apple said in a Polish accent. "All over the world."

"Not at all."

"In fack, he haf to leave here because of fans. Big crowds. He go to other motel."

John Bark asked a fast, "Which one?"

"Dunno," Apple said. "Me, I'm only the janitor in dis here place."

"Don't worry, I'll find out."

As he walked on at a trudge, Apple wondered which had the most value, his inventiveness or that instant response to danger.

On looking down while climbing iron stairs to the exterior walkway, Apple saw no signs of English fan Bark. He hoped that situation would obtain over the following days. Complications he didn't need.

The upper level's end unit, the Royal Suite, was without lights, so Apple gave his intentions to a siesta rather than to Bull Massive. In any case, he had come close to deciding that his purpose might be best served by keeping his distance from the wrestler socially.

In his own unit Apple lay on the bed, on his back. He used the Japanese system—thumbs behind the ears and forefinger-tips in the nostrils. Trouble was, every time he started to doze off, his hands slid out of position.

Apple was glad no one was there to see; glad that he had actually slept that last time, which was better than baldly admitting that some of the things they taught you in the spy game just didn't work.

Not looking at his watch Apple got up and went to shower. Half an hour later, clean and sharp and yawning, he drove away from the motel in his rented car.

Parking downtown, Apple went to the service lane beside Empress Hall, which was in heavy darkness down one side, the other lit from the distant stage-door's naked bulb. It was a vista melodramatic enough to make Apple sigh with satisfaction.

He wasn't in the least surprised when, at the lane's midway point, he heard a sinister hiss. It came, he saw as he peered at the dark side, from a small figure. He went across. Not to have done so would have been an act of self-denial he could not have accomplished.

The figure was male, fifty years old and dressed in genteel shabbiness. Under a Nero fringe he had a sad, scholarly face. He looked like a poet who didn't want anyone to know he made a good living at it.

"I got a message for ya, kid," he said.

Apple, politely: "From whom?"

"From me, like, if you're one of the rasslers."

"I am."

"Okay, kid. I'm Knotty. Everyone knows Knotty. I got the best goods in the East."

"That's nice," Apple said.

"Steroids, coke, crack, acid—I got 'em."

"I see."

"If you want soft drugs—forget it. Knotty don't fool with that baby stuff."

"Point taken."

The little man asked, "So what can I serve you with this evening, kid?"

After explaining that he was well supplied for the moment, thank you, and shaking Knotty's furtive hand in gratitude, Apple went on. Having met someone who was truly slimy, he felt delighted, for himself and for his future biography, and for the seed of an idea.

With a glance behind to see his shadow stretched out ominously, Apple mused: *It was in a wretched alley late at night that agent Porter first met the notorious drug baron whose name, even now, can not be placed in the public domain for fear of reprisal.*

Better that way than using the name the little man went by, Apple agreed, which was more cute than tough. A certain amount of poetic licence would have to be allowed.

Smiling because of his conviction that he possessed not a shred of discomfort, Apple walked on.

"Silver Flash!"

The crowd responded well to the introduction, considering it had just seen an exciting, emotion-draining bout, which Apple, now in wrestling gear, had watched from the rear seats. So hard had he pulled for the victim to fight back that he had kicked himself in the ankle.

Now Apple limped forward from his corner of the ring, arm raised, stirred by the moment's glamour. He went on circling until the referee said, "Do you mind?"

The other wrestler, introduced next, was Batter Brown. His short fat body had a fluff of hair that thickened on his face and head. At intro's end, he merely gazed around with a deep, well-performed scowl.

Apple's attention was mostly at ringside, where sat the ripe Agnes de Grace, in the same seat as before. Her outfit was bright screaming green. Whether or not her panties matched, Apple as yet had been unable to fathom, the position of her legs being inconvenient.

Apple caught the blonde looking up at him. He bowed. She turned away, but the matrons on either side of her waved with glee. You're doing great, One, Apple thought with reluctance, remembering the caper.

This made him thrust all his attention to the business at hand, as a bell rang to start the bout. He told himself he was going to be one of the fastest losers in the checkered history of professional wrestling.

Someone catcalled, "Give him a slash, Flash!"

While other clever snatches of verse sounded above the laughter, Apple and Batter Brown stalked around each other in their crouches. They swapped glares. They hissed like fishwives struck dumb.

Batter Brown rushed forward. Apple, on realising he had neatly sidestepped, was furious. He advised himself to ignore instinct, be amenable, accept defeat as a thing of honour.

Further, facing his opponent again, Apple told himself to use a Zola's Charge, also known as a Jack Hughs. When it didn't work, you finished up flat on your back, winded, unable to prevent yourself from being pinned.

A flash of movement at ringside entered the corner of Apple's eye. He swung his head around to look. The long legs of Agnes de Grace, in the act of crossing, allowed a glimpse of nether green.

The lights went out.

In the darkness there was peace. Apple floated happily and smoothly. He knew he was in paradise and as far as he was concerned paradise was fine; he had a good mind to take up permanent residence.

When the silence began to be punctured by voices, Apple murmured a complaint, then another as the darkness started to grow specks and shafts of light.

He became groggily conscious. There were faces above him, a crowd's roar in the background. He remembered where he was. With surprise and a niggle of pride he realised he had been knocked out.

Next he felt himself being lifted upright, helped out of the ring and semi-carried. All was a confusion which gradually cleared until he was standing alert in the shower. The nape of his neck hurt.

Brilliant, he mused. Out for the count and out of the competition. Well done, One.

As Apple left the showers a man called, "Congrats." It gave Apple pause, a condition that lingered as others in the dressing room called out similars and one came across to slap his shoulder, with, "You're doing okay, S.F."

Apple stopped the man from moving on. "I'm still

dizzy," he said. "Could you tell me what happened exactly."

"Sure. Batter Brown was disqualified."

"He was?"

"For fouling you. It was a forearm smash to the back of the neck, a rabbit punch."

Ten minutes later, dressed in street clothes, Apple was still absorbing the annoying/titillating news that he had won the match, that a blow meant for the side of his neck had gone astray as he turned to look at Agnes de Grace, when a uniformed usher came in the room and over to the bench.

"Note for you, Mr. Flash," he said, handing the envelope over. "Could I have your autograph instead of a tip, please?"

That arranged, Apple the while humming lightly, he sat down to read the note. It was from Agnes de Grace. She said it would give her great pleasure if Silver Flash would meet her as soon as possible. She was sitting in a white stretch limo parked in front of Empress Hall.

Head lowered, Apple shot glances at the other men present. They had none of that rigid casualness, he reckoned, that tells of conspiracy, a gag, or a practical joke, but that still didn't mean the note was kosher. The jester could be elsewhere.

Even so, Apple hustled in leaving the changing room and getting to the street out front. Standing there was a white stretch limousine with dark glass. Apple went across and stooped to look in the rear. It was empty.

There came a blast on the car horn. It made Apple first jump nervously, and then look into the front. Sitting behind the steering wheel was Agnes de Grace.

Apple said, "Hello."

"You got my note, I see."

"Yes. Thank you."

"Jump in, darling."

"Yes," Apple said, not quite honouring that verb in entering the front but doing it no disservice either.

"I gave my chauffeur the week off," the blonde said in a voice like hot smoke. "How do you do."

"How do you do."

"So meaningful to meet you."

"I feel exactly the same, Ms. de Grace."

"Call me Aggers, darling."

"Thank you," Apple said. "Please call me Edward."

"Is it your name?"

"Edward Parker, yes, of Manchester."

"Well, Edward, you look quite charming out of your mask."

"Nice of you to say so."

"Off we go," Agnes de Grace said, starting the motor. She shot away from the curb directly into the path of a man on a pedal bicycle. He braked, wobbled, yelled—and fell off.

Driving on, Agnes de Grace said, "The poor can be such a menace, can't they?"

"Oh yes," Apple said. At this moment he would have agreed that black and white were red, being heady with the blonde's luxurious, voluptuous presence. Breathing in deeply through his nose he decided she had the aroma of hot buttered toast with lemon marmalade.

And yet, one small sane part of his mind was carefully registering a callousness which had a message of hope for him in respect of the mission; though half of that small part was warning about appearances not always being what they seemed: the callous bit could be as phony as the cliché *darling,* all part of the movie star image.

As was, Apple assumed, the disco music that came blasting out of spread speakers after the driver had pressed a button. His ears would have hurt if he hadn't been so intrigued. In a way, he was glad the noise made speech impossible; they might have ruined everything with a chat about the weather.

Driving swiftly, Agnes de Grace soon reached suburbs. She steered between trees, then brought the limousine to a stop, killing motor and lights. Beyond the windows lay pitch darkness; inside there was a low glow from the dashboard.

When the music had also been switched off, Apple asked, "Where's this, Aggers?"

"Local lovers' lane, darling," Agnes de Grace said. "We can have a talk here without being disturbed."

"How convenient."

"Let's get in the back, shall we?"

"I simply had to talk to you, Edward, after what you went through with that Batter Brown. The animal."

Apple said, "Well, I don't think the rabbit punch was *really* intentional."

"Oh, but darling."

"I have an idea I turned to look at something."

"What?"

Even in the gloom Apple could see that Agnes de Grace was now wearing stockings. They were green like everything else. Her legs were nearest, as she was semi-kneeling sideways on the seat.

Apple said, "I was looking at you, Aggers, as a matter of absolute fact."

"Flatterer," the actress drawled, smiling in a shy way. "But I believe you totally."

"I can't think of anything I'd rather look at."

"Darling."

"I've called your home several times. I told the girl there I was a secret admirer."

"Oh, that was *you.* How very sweet. I love it that you've called eighteen times at last count and that, I'm told, you keep using different voices."

Weakly: "I'm a card."

"I'm sure you are, darling," Agnes de Grace said, patting his arm. "You have that look in your eye." She edged closer, a green knee almost touching his leg. "Now, Edward. I want to know all about you. Your life. Childhood. Education. Marital status. Birthmarks."

Apple, who had been on the verge of adding that last one himself, as a witticism with a risqué quality, said a kind, "That's very funny, Aggers."

"I mean it, darling. I want to know every single thing. I'm fascinated. Go on."

He went on. What he didn't know about his cover person he invented. This meant that ninety percent of what he said was born of imagination, he told himself. In reality the details were borrowed from a score of books, beginning with *Tom Brown's Schooldays.*

Apple was happily distraught. While he talked, Agnes de Grace, who had shuffled closer yet, responded to salient points in the saga by patting his shoulder, tapping his thigh or giving his forearm gentle squeezes.

When Apple concluded with his entry into the world of professional wrestling, the actress stroked the back of his neck slowly and lightly. She said:

"What a fascinating life you've had, darling. The drama. The risk. Drilling for oil in the Sahara, mountaineering, almost fighting a duel in Paris, car racing. By comparison, my life has been monotonous."

"I'm sure that isn't true, Aggers."

"I do tend to exaggerate."

Apple said, "Please tell me about yourself."

"I'd adore to," Agnes de Grace said like a cat mewing for more. "But first I must get comfortable." Swinging her legs smoothly down off the seat, she turned away. "Get the zip for me, will you, darling?"

"The—er—zip?"

"Pull it down."

Humming to give the impression he was no stranger to this sort of thing, Apple took a hold on the fastener and lowered it to the waist. He had supposed that was the end, that the dress had been rendered less tight above, but he was wrong.

Agnes de Grace, facing front, pulled the green garment forward and down, eased it from around and under her hips, pushed it to the floor and took it off.

Languid as a tired orchid, she leaned back in the seat corner. She was a study in green, with pink flesh showing where there were no shoes, sheer stockings, garter-belt, panties, bra.

Apple asked creakily, "Better?"

Nodding graciously, Agnes de Grace started to talk of her childhood out on the prairies. To Apple it could have been the most fantastic story he had ever heard and he still wouldn't have cared. He was far more taken by the elegant, leg-waving way the narrator heeled off one shoe and then the other.

It was while she was telling about the occasion when, to stay off school so she could knit socks for orphans, she had lied, claiming to have a headache, that the blonde delicately unhooked her left stocking. She caressed it down her leg, wheedled it off her foot.

Some minutes later she did the same on the other side. It was during her recounting of how, on her first date, she had let the boy hold her hand; and worse, how she hadn't mentioned a word of it to her mother afterwards.

Apple tried to look more shocked than the way he had during the headache confession. His features again failing to cooperate, he said, "Oh dear."

Busy tying her stocking with its mate around the door-handle, Agnes de Grace said, "We all have these regrets."

"Yes indeed."

The actress leaned upright. As she reached both hands behind her, she started telling about how she had altered a photocopy of her birth certificate in order to get into drama school. She had been seventeen, not eighteen.

"Ah well," Apple said, shaking his head though his eyes never left the green bra.

Her hands evidently busy behind, the blonde said, "I'm not ashamed of that incident, I admit." She went on to talk of ways and means. "So there," she finished, at the same time bringing her hands back to the front and with them the bra's ends. She let the article fall off, and brushed it aside.

As though in relief at finding freedom, her breasts moved gently until Agnes de Grace had finished settling. She reclined like a Goya model in the corner, one arm crooked behind her head.

"Absolutely fascinating," Apple mumbled, full of respect for the quality on display.

"No life, darling, can be completely without fascination," the actress murmured, smiling into his eyes.

"True. Quite true. Very true. True."

"For instance there was the time when cousin Philip and I went to the Olympic Games."

Although he did register that her cousin's name had cropped up before, more than once, Apple failed to follow the story, so consumed was he by watching the storyteller's hand. It seemed to have a life of its own.

At a flowing, leisurely pace the hand was moving to the green panties. It began edging them down off the garter-belt. The silken materials whispered together in quiet conspiracy.

Trying, as always, to do the right thing, Apple shared his delighted attention between the generous breasts and the descending drawers.

With true blonde Agnes de Grace still talking, her cheeky hand got the panties lowered to her knees. The other hand came down to help and the flimsy garment was removed.

Apple sighed.

The actress said, "Yes, it was sad, a poor start to his career. But we have high hopes that it's going to end the complete reverse of that."

Trying to attend: "Oh yes?"

"The Festival will probably be Philip's swan song. What with advancing years, rheumatism and one thing and another. He's going to retire."

Trying, trying: "Festival? Philip?"

"Yes, darling. My cousin. He wrestles professionally as Mad Mountain Phil."

"That's a coincidence."

"What is?"

"He's my next opponent."

"Really?"

"We have a bout tomorrow night."

Agnes de Grace started to unfasten her garter-belt. She said a plaintive, "It would be tragic if poor Philip didn't reach at least the semi-finals."

"Oh, I'm sure he will," Apple said. "For positive, I don't stand a chance against him."

"You don't, darling?"

"Not a ghost of one."

The blonde drew off her garter-belt and dropped it to the floor. Stretching her nakedness tautly and sitting tall, she said, "How good it feels to get out of those confining undies."

"Yes," Apple said. "Yes."

After a glance toward the dashboard, Agnes de Grace said, "Goodness me, look at the time."

"What?"

"I must fly."

"What?"

"I'm expecting a call from Hollywood."

"What?"

Picking up her dress, the blonde began to pull it on over her legs, the while saying, "Perhaps, darling, we could meet again tomorrow evening, right after your bout with Philip. Same spot. We could go out to my place, have an intimate little supper, just the two of us. What d'you say?"

"Well . . ."

Turning her back, dress on: "Please zip me up, darling."

Although the sports section of the morning paper, the *Toronto Sphere & Post,* reserved its headline for Bull Massive's victory yesterday afternoon, a sub-banner spoke about a second dubious win for Silver Flash. Underneath his photograph (lying unconscious) it asked, "Could the popular English wrestler be the Festival sleeper?"

Popular; Apple liked that. It made up for the photograph, which he considered poor taste. He refolded the newspaper so the picture couldn't be seen before he started reading the Silver Flash piece again, for the third time. He read while continuing with his breakfast in the motel coffee shop, which had sparse custom, the morning being well advanced.

"Could I borrow the ketchup, please?"

"Of course." Reaching for the bottle, Apple looked up. His hand he drew back when he saw who the man was. "No, you couldn't."

"I didn't want it anyway," Chuck said with a tug on the peak of his yachting cap. "My table has two bottles."

"Nor are you hounding me at every turn. Your being here is pure coincidence."

"You're astute, One. I have to hand you that."

"So long," Apple said. "It's been fun."

Chuck said, "I just stopped by to congratulate you on the great way you're managing to keep that low profile." He turned and left, humming off-key.

Apple told himself he couldn't stand envious people, and went on with his eating and reading. Once he broke off to look around, to locate the agent and, if the coast was clear, give him a sociable nod. But Chuck had left.

Article finished, Apple with no pause replayed the paragraph he had toyed with casually this morning:

As the blonde beauty slowly disrobed, removing every last item of clothing until she was nude, agent Porter sat there cool and in charge of matters, his trained mind looking beyond this moment.

Wishing he hadn't bothered with the replay, Apple chewed grumpily. He was forced to grant audience to what had been nagging for attention since last night, when the actress had dropped him off at the Puck.

Were there motives? In the actions and words of Agnes de Grace had there been a suggestion of bribery? Or had that limo scene simply been what it seemed: an adult woman having the sense to get comfortable, knowing by the cut of his jib that the person she was with was a man of the world who would not get the wrong impression; a woman who had a perfectly valid reason for rushing away—Hollywood was important to her.

There had been, Apple acknowledged, a hint that on their next meeting (date, you could say) they would become more intimate, but that was surely normal for a mature, sophisticated lady who had taken a shine to the virile, victorious athlete. There was no reason to suspect Aggers of suggesting that if her cousin Philip were allowed to win, the loser would receive sexual favours.

The audience was over. Suspicion never had a chance against Apple's rare, Festival-tickled vanity. He certainly did not think that what he ought to do was arrange for a camera or tape-recorder to be snooping while he tried to get Agnes de Grace to state outright her terms in connexion with any possible corruption.

Apple reminded himself that he had already assured the lady her cousin would be a winner; nothing could be truer. To lose the match this evening, Mad Mountain Phil would have to be truly feeling his advancing age and be petrified by his rheumatism.

Breakfast over, Apple went out to his car. The newspaper he put under the seat, along with a reminder to clip out the pertinent piece later, to add to his collection of mission souvenirs. He reflected, with passing bitterness, that it must be the smallest collection extant.

Apple drove off and away from town. Environs he already knew from his day-one familiarisation excursion, which included locating the rented house of Agnes de Grace.

But Apple didn't want to dwell on the luscious blonde. He wished to be agent Porter, cool and in charge. Patience was a virtue and he was going to be saintly in not thinking about tonight, not recalling that body, those gregarious breasts, that smiling navel, those luscious thighs, those dimpled knees . . .

Seeing he had gone too far, Apple made a U-turn and went back. He had to slow because of the dust he had raised on the gravel road that ran rod-straight between trees. There were no other vehicles around, standing or moving.

After stopping, Apple checked his watch. His timing was excellent. He got out of the car but left its motor ticking over and its door unlatched.

That he might be encouraging theft, thereby helping crime to flower, Apple put aside in favour of the more exciting idea of an escaped convict coming across this gift.

He went into the trees at one side. After a dozen metres, the long strip of woodland thinned, and a golf course came into view. To the left lay a green, to the right men could be seen slowly approaching a tee. There were eight men; four golfers and their caddies.

After getting himself level with the nearby green,

Apple kept out of sight, crouching and peering for the spyness of it. Down at the tee, one golfer struck off. His ball landed on the green's far rim.

Next, Samuel Glacier took his swing. Conveniently, the ball came to a stop just before the circle, in tufty grass. Apple waited.

He waited until, the other pair having shot, the group had started walking this way. He lay down flat and wriggled out of the trees. Although he wasn't hidden from the group, he assured himself he wouldn't stand out in his greenish shirt and slacks.

With a final wriggle and a stretch of long arm, Apple got the ball. Reversing, he reached and penetrated the trees. Upright again, he chose a thick trunk to stand behind.

The men ambled along, coming abreast out there in the open. Samuel Glacier said, "Hey, I was sure my pill landed right here." His caddy agreed. The other players made curious sing-song noises, said to start searching in the woods, and asked if the wager was too high.

Tailed by his caddy, Samuel Glacier came into the trees. Apple tossed the ball toward him. It landed with a clatter among the leaves of autumn.

The gambler frowned, glanced all around, went to the landing point, saw his ball. While he was bending, Apple crouched clear of the tree in order to throw out onto the green, toward its cup, the ball he had bought yesterday.

Several things happened at once. Some of the other men started calling out to know what the hell was going on here. Samuel Glacier straightened. Apple failed to get himself fully back out of sight. Briefly, before he swung away, he and Glacier looked at each other.

The caddy shouted, "It's one'a them ball thieves."

Apple ran. He charged between trunks toward what his mind had designated the get-away vehicle. That he himself might have created via poor physical coordination the need to make a fast escape he was treating as curtly as he was his relieved knowledge that the ploy, even if it worked, which it seemed to have done, would do little harm to the gambler, who might be the straightest man in the world. What Apple did fondle was the undoubted fact that he had done something positive for the mission.

Panting with success and exertion, Apple reached the car, slammed inside and sped off. The get-away, with wheels spinning and motor ranting, could have been no more dramatic if the pursuit had consisted of six heavies with guns instead of one middle-aged caddie waving a number 2 iron.

Apple got his idea following lunch (steak and salad). On leaving the downtown restaurant he saw Knotty. The dope dealer, looking like a defrocked priest, was entering an alley across the street.

Yes, Apple mused. We obtain the goods, we plant same on the subject after alerting the police, we finger him for arrest. One of the Trio down and two to go.

It was a brilliant idea, Apple had to admit, while not going so far as to wonder why he hadn't thought of it earlier, but helping out by musing how far from obvious it was.

The goods he would not, of course, obtain from Knotty, Apple figured. He wasn't about to get involved with illegal doings. The answer was the ubiquitous Chuck.

"Excuse me, sir."

Apple stopped at once, stabbed in spirit as always when being given a title. His mind fretted—Am I getting old?—even as he was taking in the tall crew-cutted man in sports coat and rakish bow-tie. "Yes?"

"Are you Silver Flash, by any chance?"

"Er, Silver Flash?"

"Yes, the wrestler. You know who I mean."

"I don't know what makes you think I do."

Young, pink faced, earnest, the man said, "You must be part of the Festival."

"And you must be an autograph hound."

"No no no, nothing like that."

"Fan?"

Swinging up on his toes, which made him nearly as tall as Apple, the stranger said, "I'm Walter Bane of the *Post.* Everyone calls me Speedy."

Apple took a wary step backward. He snapped the fingers of both hands, alternately, an attention-distracting gimmick from Training Three, while he decided on another gimmick, from Training Five. It was one of several available on how to get rid of a reporter: offer to sell him the story of your life.

"It was inevitable that we should meet like this," Apple said, moving forward again with fingers still. "I came here on impulse, Speedy. If I may call you that."

"Sure."

"And for the first time ever I meet a genuine newspaperman. The strange twists of fate, eh?"

He said droningly, "You are not Silver Flash."

"My name's Albert Watkin. I'm a plumber. I've had

a fascinating life, as my mother could tell you, and it would make a marvellous series for a newspaper."

"Yes," Speedy Bane said absently, looking around.

"Later it could be done in book form."

"Sure thing. But I have to be running."

Apple said, "I don't want a fortune for it."

Backing off, he said, "Good."

"As my mother says, the world ought to know this story of a simple man who was determined to become a master plumber and serve people."

Blinking, Speedy Bane said, "It does sound kinda human interest stuff. I mean, plumbers get around."

Coldly: "Oh?"

"Why don't you tell me a couple of the highlights, Albert? You do any plumbing in prisons, brothels, offices of politicians? You do much work in the homes of the famous?"

"There goes Mumble," Apple said, waving at a gap in the distance. "Let's get together real soon." He went off at a fast stride and didn't look back.

Five minutes later, Apple went into a drug store and used the telephone. The number he dialled he had memorised days ago. With a finger in one ear against background noise (it was a wall phone) he heard a female voice ask for identification. He gave a series of letters.

"Okay, One," the woman said cheerily. "What's up?"

"I need something."

"We are here but to serve."

"Fine. I'd like to be served with a small amount of a drug. Heroin, I think."

"How small?"

"The packet should be slim enough to slip into a

person's pocket, the amount of dope should be large enough to constitute a crime, for possession."

"I'll pass that along."

"It would be nice if it could be delivered to me inside the next two hours."

The woman asked, "Where?"

"Give it to Chuck," Apple said. "I'm sure he'll know where to find me. Over and out."

This glibness would have made Apple come close to blushing if he hadn't had other matters on his mind. But, as he crossed to the soda fountain, he reminded himself that the true pro operatives always played it casual.

At the counter Apple had a coffee. He returned to the telephone, taking along a balled piece of paper napkin so he wouldn't be seen standing there with a finger in his ear, and which was the real reason he had gone for a coffee in the first place.

Ball prodded deep, Apple dialled the Puck Motel. He asked to be connected with the Royal Suite. The girl at the desk said, "Mr. Massive isn't in his unit."

"Any idea where he might be?"

"Yes."

"Good—where?"

The girl said, "He's in the restaurant here having lunch."

"Great. Could you please have him come to the phone. I have a message for him from Mr. Glacier."

After a lingering silence the wrestler came on the line. He said, "If Mr. Glacier has a message for me why doesn't he give it to me personally?"

"Beg pardon?"

"We're having lunch together."

Apple blurted, "I don't believe it." What he meant

was, things like this shouldn't happen. About to hang up, he held back on hearing Bull Massive say:

"Okay. Sorry about that."

"I don't understand."

"I get lotsa nuisance calls, people using friends' names to make contact. Forget it. What's the message?"

Apple smiled as he said, "Mr. Glacier wonders if you could meet him at four o'clock in the Hockey Lounge of the Wexford."

"Guess so," the wrestler said.

Leaving the drug store, Apple rubbed mental hands at how well he was doing, including that bluff. He didn't dwell on the possibility of Bull Massive contacting Samuel Glacier or meeting him by accident because things like that also shouldn't, and generally didn't, happen.

Going into another store, Apple asked to see some sunglasses. The girl clerk whispered at him. He said, "What's that?" She whispered again, leaning forward across the counter.

Also leaning, Apple asked, "Sore throat?"

The girl said a quiet, "No, I always speak loudly."

In time, before he got nervous, Apple remembered. He dug the ball of paper out of his ear, explaining, "Cotton. I've had an infection."

"It's going around, sir," the girl said. "What price range sunglasses do you want?"

Apple put on his new glasses as he crossed Emperor Avenue. They had been the most expensive pair in the store and he was disappointed at not feeling discomforted by this shameless misuse of Upstairs funds. However, his obviously growing cynicism was a sop.

He entered a bowling alley. The dark glasses he had

to take off, unable to see if people were looking at him suspiciously when he was unsure if they were looking at him at all.

After getting pop from a machine, Apple sat at a table. Sipping, he played rapt spectator while enjoying the knowledge that no one knew he was sitting here waiting to score some horse.

Although this enjoyment had long palled by the passing of an hour, Apple got pleasure out of playing it cool when Chuck came in and sat at the table.

"Hi, One."

"You have the goods?"

"Sure thing. Let's slip to the head."

"Of course not. Just put the packet right out on the table here. What curious ideas you have."

Apple stopped outside the cocktail lounge to straighten his cap. Bright blue, of the baseball variety, it said whitely on the front, EMPIRE. They were being worn by many of the tourists in town, though not, naturally, by any of the locals. In his low-pulled cap and his sunglasses, Apple felt safe from recognition by anyone who had seen him before only casually.

He went on in to the Hockey Lounge. It was expansive, carpeted, bearing all the soft touches that went with olives and swizzlesticks and dishes of nuts. It was a quiet time of day, and the tables had few patrons. The long bar had a mere half dozen proppers, one of whom was Bull Massive.

Wearing a red blazer, lights shining on his hairless head, the wrestler stood in profile talking to an older woman and the bartender.

Apple crossed the room. Humming to show his innocence, yet doing it quietly so as not to be heard and attract attention to himself, he sidled into position directly beside Bull Massive's broad back.

As the barman glanced over with eyebrows raised, Apple ordered a tomato juice. The older woman, her kind face firm, went on telling the wrestler how in his bout tonight he should go about reducing his opponent to bloody rubble.

Apple's drink came. He paid, left his change on the bar alongside the tomato juice to reserve his all-important place, then hummed his way out of the lounge.

The hotel lobby's four cowl telephones were engaged. But even as Apple slowed at the sight, one of the callers moved away. Telling himself what an excellent omen this was, how smoothly everything would now develop, Apple went to the empty place at a swift walk.

When he was connected with the police station he said, in a whining tone, "Listen, there's some guy in the bar here what's carrying heroin."

"What bar?"

"I don't know if it's for his own self or if he's selling it, but he's got it right enough."

"What bar?"

"He's one'a them rasslers. Famous, I bet. Ought to be put behind bars, goddam drug attic."

"What bar?"

"Oh, and one more thing, the bar he's in's called the Hockey Lounge. You boys'd best hurry."

"Your name, sir?"

"Think I want to get my head bent?" Apple asked as if amazed. He disconnected.

Tensing at the approach of a moment of truth, he headed back. Could he do it?—he questioned. Did he retain any of the skill he had been taught for that mission he thought of as the Case of the Hungry Diplomat?

Getting a gram of calm from trying to recall the name of the man who had coached him in the basics of pickpocketing, a suitable impossibility, Apple returned to his place by Bull Massive's back. Everything and everyone was as before. The woman was in favour of eye-gouging.

Leaving the search for a name until later, Apple set events in motion. He reckoned he had less than five minutes.

His fingertips he rubbed rapidly on the bar's underlip, thus creating a hot tingle with an aftermath of increased sensitivity. Dipping into his own pocket he brought out in the palm of his hand a white paper parcel the size and shape of a squashed cigarette pack. He shuffled around until he was standing close behind Bull Massive and staring at the back of his neck.

To boost confidence by feeding ego, as taught, Apple recalled his cleverness in making the rendezvous a cocktail lounge, where a man would be sure to wear some kind of jacket; loose fitting and with pockets.

Apple noted with a minor start that he was being stared at by the bartender, a thin person with a white nose. However, before Apple could purse his lips in a whistle the barman looked back at the kind-faced matron, who had said, "You have to tear the bastard's arm out."

Bull Massive said, "I'll do my best."

Barman: "There's nothing finer."

The left pocket on the wrestler's blazer was agape. With the greatest of ease, Apple slipped the heroin into it.

He stepped back, coughed, swung smartly to the

bar, lifted his glass. He sipped. Celebration drink over, he began to amble away, tomato juice in hand. He froze when the barkeep said, "Just a moment."

Apple turned only midway, hunching. "Yes?"

"Don't forget your change."

"Ah. Keep it."

Collection accomplished, albeit untidily, Apple made his way to a table near the entrance, open double-doors, from where he could watch the proceedings, which—his own production—he wouldn't have missed for a height reduction of one inch. He looked at his watch.

Over at the bar a moment later, Bull Massive did the same. He said, "Just after four. That means he isn't coming."

Woman: "Who?"

"Someone I was supposed to meet here at four o'clock. So I guess I'll mosey."

"Why? He's hardly even late yet."

"My friend's one of those people that's always ten minutes early for any date."

"Well, in that case," the woman said.

Apple dithered on one leg. He willed, *Don't go.*

Bull Massive stood erect, stretched his mighty arms, and said, "Been nice seeing you, Min. You too, Hap."

While Bull Massive began to back away, Apple went on dithering, chewed the inside of his lip and listened for the police siren, which he knew very well would not be used in a situation such as this.

The wrestler was patting himself, as leavers do. He said, "Guess I got a nuisance call after all." He continued patting, moving down his blazer.

"Price of fame," the woman said.

Bartender: "Expensive."

Bull Massive held in mid-pat and stopped reversing away. He said, "Hold on."

Apple ended his dither, his chew and his listen. With a quick glance aside he measured the distance between the exit and himself.

Bull Massive dropped his hands. Moving back toward the bar he said, "I'm being stupid, come to think of it."

Bartender: "Yeah?"

"Why should it have been a nuisance call? Even if my buddy's never been late in his life there's always a first time, for any of a hundred reasons."

"Right," the woman said.

Apple relaxed.

The wrestler was saying how impatient everyone was in this modern era. "And to excuse ourselves, we jump to conclusions. There I was all ready to malign that unknown caller."

Woman and barkeep: "Sure."

"I mean, whatever happened to trust?"

Apple stopped feeling relaxed. He was distinctly uncomfortable. He realised he had been so preoccupied with the mechanics of his campaign and the reverse dip that he hadn't paused to consider the moral aspect.

He did so now. Or anyway, he tried to. There was nothing to consider, he saw. He had been one hundred percent immoral. He had set up for arrest, trial, public disdain and imprisonment a man who was probably quite decent; a man reputed to be a good husband; a man known to be a loving father to his five children, youngsters who would not be allowed to visit him in prison; a man of trust and sensitivity who . . .

Bull Massive said, "I'll give it a few more minutes."

Apple got up. Children, a woman, a convict—idealised pictures of these made him move at a sleepwalker plod back to the bar, where he again took up a position behind the wrestler, who was talking about that little bit of good there seemed to be in everyone.

The fact of him having brought along his drink, which he now noticed, let Apple know he was operating on all mental cylinders, not motivated (solely) by foolish sentiment and the wild exaggerations of imagination.

He limbered up his hand with rubs and clenches. The guilty blazer pocket was on the bar side, as before, but no longer had its gape, Bull Massive being in a different stance.

From behind, at the door, came a flurry of arrival. Fearfully, Apple snatched his head around. He quivered on seeing two women, who headed for a distant table.

Knowing he could wait no longer, Apple made his move. In approved professional style he nudged the wrestler's back with an elbow while mumbling an excuse-me and thrusting two long fingers into that pocket.

Bull Massive's awareness being on the heavier of the two contacts—the nudge—he paid little heed to the other. The apology he nodded off over his shoulder.

Delicately, Apple withdrew his two-finger pincer, which held the small white package. By telling himself to go ahead and drop it, great, fabulous, he managed not to. The heroin he got safely into his pocket.

Following a pause for recovery and another sip of tomato juice, Apple sidled away, glass in hand. Again he hummed for his own ears only. He was almost back at his table when the two men came in at a bustle. They looked excited enough to start bouncing.

One of the police officers was in uniform. The other wore plain clothes of so official a stamp that he might as well have been in uniform anyway. After a swift glance around they marched to the bar, to the bald wrestler.

Sitting, leaning back, folding his arms, Apple observed the scene with smug eyes. Everyone else in the cocktail lounge was likewise attentive.

Courteously, apologetically, the plain-clothes man explained to Bull Massive about the anonymous telephone call. Laughing, the woman and the barman shook their heads.

Also laughing, the wrestler said, "If your anonymous fink meant me, officer, he's mistaken."

Detective: "Mind if we search you, sir?"

"Mind? Hell, I insist."

The search, brief but thorough, produced nothing. The detective said, "Sorry about that, Mr. Massive."

The woman said, "I should think so."

The bartender said, so quietly that Apple only just heard, "The guy over there could be a wrestler."

Apple became the horrified focal point of every eye in the bar group. He creaked up out of his big-boss slouch. He rose to his feet. He moved toward the door. He snapped into a stride when the detective called, "One moment, please."

THREE

As he crossed the hotel lobby, threading his way through a goodly crowd, Apple settled to a running walk. This he did with consummate skill, having had a lifetime of practice in the art of making himself less noticeable than necessary when among people.

His upper body appeared fairly normal, but from the hips down it was different. His bent legs were revolving at speed, like someone who didn't want to admit to himself how urgently he needed to get to the latrine.

Exit drawing closer, Apple glanced back, popping up to his true height to see better. The two policemen had come out of the lounge and were grimly in pursuit.

Confident of getting away once he was outdoors, Apple bragged inwardly to hide the falseness of his confidence that this would make his third narrow escape in one day. He thought it unworthy of mention that one was from a caddy and the other from a reporter. Escapes were escapes.

After circling a final knot of people on the threshold, Apple reached the door. He dashed out onto the hotel's frontage, on Emperor Avenue.

At once he came to an arm-wheeling, forward-lurching, stiff-legged halt. Also, in case it would do any good, he put on a grin.

One of the two uniformed policemen was standing beside his motor-cycle; the other leaned on the front of his patrol car. Both officers, at Apple's advent, were alerted tautly, like gunfighters in fiction's view of the Old West. His grin made them glare.

Not waiting to see what happened next, Apple, balance recovered, said disarmingly as he swung around, "They're on their way out so don't leave."

He dashed back inside.

His pursuers were there, forging through the people knot, plain-clothes detective in the lead. He saw Apple and called out a strident:

"Halt in the name of the law!"

The knot skirmished in alarm, thus forming a trap for the policemen.

Apple circled at a stoop to head back across the lobby. Assuring himself that yes, the man had actually said that, he went into his running walk. People nearby looked at him as if annoyed at being distracted from their tip-toe stares to see what that commotion was by the door.

Apple was apprehensive about the situation, but not distraught. While he knew his arrest could be fixed from above, it would A, be a long process, taking up perhaps several days; B, be breaking one of an espionage operative's platinum rules: Never get involved with the regular police; C, be a bore; D, be a discomfort because of the way the officers would look at him in dull reproach when they had to let him go.

Therefore capture was out, Apple mused as he planned his route.

There were several exits from the lobby but most

would be dead-ends, he reckoned, such as the cocktail lounge. It would be best to take the stairs and find a quiet place to safely get rid of the heroin.

Apple looked behind him. The uniformed officer of the first pair, a sergeant, coming at a good pace, was also looking behind himself. When he turned from the knot-bound detective he wore on his face as much smugness as determination.

Or he was determined to increase his smugness, Apple thought nervously as he hurried on, knowing as he did that the most dangerous adversaries were those with personal motives.

He leapt onto the stairs and charged up. In turning the bend to leave the lobby out of sight, he noted that his closest pursuer seemed to have gained ground but that the other officers had stayed outside.

On the level, Apple ran in front of the elevators (all closed) and started up the next flight. He was beginning to question whether this had been such a bright idea after all. What if he got trapped on the top floor?

Coming onto the next level, Apple saw hope: one of the elevators stood open. Its sole occupant, an old woman in black, was reaching out to the control panel. She drew back with a gasp when Apple sprang inside.

He jabbed a button. It was bottom man on the list. With pleasing swiftness the doors closed. The cage jerked on its way downward.

Softly, the old woman said, "I wanted to go up."

Apple shuffled around to face her, aghast. He saw the wounded expression, the disappointment, the frailness—and he was attacked by a vicious blush.

With a burst of cerebral action Apple imagined himself suspended above a cauldron of molten lead on a length of frayed rope while dressed in arctic survivals.

This was the latest in a long series of antidotes for blushing. Apple got them mostly from magazine advertisements and found them good for two or three outings, before familiarity bred contempt in his emotions.

He was still impressed by the short-term cure bought by mail from Nurse Sharples of Whitechapel; still cowed weak before the superior heat and danger of the imagined picture.

Apple dangled, the hot lead smoked, the rope went on with its fraying. His painful burn cooled to a singe.

Not so much, however, that he was able to come up with an excuse to explain his gross manners to the abused party, who was pressing herself timidly against the wall. The best he could do was take his baseball cap off.

The cage stopped, and doors hissed back. Apple dove out. He was purblinded by dimness. Sunglasses removed, he saw he was in an underground garage, silent and deserted, with the exit a block of light one hundred metres distant.

Apple strode that way, following an apologetic blink at the closed elevator doors. Midway there he halted, as in through the block and down the ramp shot a blasting motor-cycle. It was ridden by the policeman from out front.

Apple was still debating moves when the officer went by, merely glancing at him as though he were void of interest, a churchgoer and taxpayer. Causation, Apple realised, came from a blending of the sudden gloom with a changed appearance—his removal of sunglasses and cap.

He ducked behind a car. Peeking, he watched the policeman come to a stop by the elevators, get off and prop his machine, leave it running, look back for the man he had just passed, start to prowl.

The moment he went from sight, Apple made the obvious move. On the balls of his feet he raced to the bike, donning cap and glasses as he went. He pushed it off its prop, jumped on, roared away and headed for the ramp. Not wishing to know how the officer was taking the humiliating theft, he didn't look back.

Up the ramp, Apple burst into daylight and swung left. There was an immediate scream of brakes: his own and those of the ex-frontage patrol car, which now rocked back from its halt six inches from the motor-bike's front wheel, its driver looking as shattered as Apple felt.

Apple recovered fast, first. He footed his machine around and drove off. Deliberately he headed for Emperor, where there would be helpful traffic. The patrol car was reversing into a complete turn.

The junction had lights. They were on yellow. Apple was distantly sorry about that but made do with leaning over severely to make the turn. The patrol car was coming right behind. They both sped along the avenue and Apple began to weave between other travelling vehicles. Behind him, the police siren came to yipping life.

Apple, hunched, divided his attention almost equally between the way ahead and what was coming at the back, his head on the constant switch. Although he didn't realise it, this ensured that neck-craners would realise who was the one being chased.

For three blocks the only thing that changed was that Apple got tired of swinging his head. In looking the other way as a sinew balance, he spotted a familiar face. It was on the opposite side of the avenue.

When a bus had gone past, Apple zipped across in a wide U-turn. He came to a stop beside the cars that were parked nose to tail, got off the bike and lay it down, leapt gallantly up onto the front of a car and down onto the sidewalk.

John Bark, the English wrestling fan, pale and pimply, said as Apple whipped off cap and glasses, "Why, hello. It's the janitor, isn't it?"

"*Ja,*" Apple said. "This a present from Silver Flash." He snapped the cap snugly onto John Bark's head and moved off. In a crouch he ran along the line of cars until the siren was behind him, when he cut through onto the road. Running across it he looked back. The policeman was striding from his car toward where the baseball-capped fan stood in bewilderment, though the stride was already faltering. Apple aimed for a movie house.

Although he hadn't seen it before, he had read the book. That wasn't the least bit important, he let himself know as he settled into the twist which tall-tall people have to employ in theatres. What mattered was he had flushed the heroin down the lavatory and could now relax and rest. It wouldn't hurt to sit again through a vapid love story about bank clerks and flat-chested teachers, even if he did know the surprise ending that redeemed it all.

Letting his head droop, Apple fell asleep.

A musical crescendo brought him awake. He bleared at the screen, where *The End* was materialising on people who looked surprised. Getting up with the audience, he scuffled out on twinging legs.

For late in the day there were an unusual number of people on the street, it seemed to Apple. As the number grew he understood; the crowd was mainly made up of cinema audience combined with spectators from the afternoon session at Empress Hall, farther along.

In the crowd Apple felt safe, even though he accepted the police couldn't be looking for him actively. They had enough on their plate this week without scouring around for someone who was merely a suspect.

Ruffled, Apple rolled his shoulders. Merely?—he mused sardonically. The suspect had led them on a merry dance in and out of cocktail lounges and lobbies and elevators, stolen a motor-bike, broken the speed limit and made an illegal U-turn. That's all.

In defence, Apple made brave by returning his height to normal from the standard sag he used almost unconsciously when in crowds. It enabled him to see on the marquee of Empress Hall the names of tonight's combatants, among them his own. Another was Bull Massive's.

Apple thought about it.

Two sharp pomps on a car horn brought around the heads of some fifty pedestrians; many of the males stopped in a glitter of insane hope. Apple's hope, even more juvenile, was that everyone would see that it was he the pomp had been meant for.

With a blasé lilt in his walk he went between cars to the tarmac and to the side of the stretch limousine. Agnes de Grace smiled up at him.

"Hello, darling."

"Hello, Aggers."

"You stand out in a crowd."

"So do you," Apple said. "Good show?"

"So-so."

While the actress talked on about her afternoon of

wrestling matches, Apple, aware of envious glares, got his position right for a sighting on her left nipple.

He said, "Wonderful."

"Well, being in the profession yourself, I suppose you see these things differently. Give you a lift?"

"To lovers' lane?"

She pouted regret. "I have to get back to the house, darling. I'm expecting another call from Hollywood. But I can wait if you can."

"Just about," Apple said, husky. Liking the sound, he said it again, and then because it traitorously came out with a high pitch he chased it with a fast, "Be neat if you could give me a ride back to the motel."

"Darling, I'd be thrilled to bits."

When they were driving off, Apple turned his head away so observers could see him. Agnes de Grace said, "I'm looking forward to tonight so much."

Proud of his subtlety in not yawning, Apple looked around meaningfully. "You and me both."

"I could watch wrestling anytime, but especially when I know the battlers real well."

"Ah yes."

"Are you feeling fit, darling?"

"Not bad, but I don't stand a chance against Mad Mountain Phil, I can assure you. Promise you."

Leaning across to pat his knee, Agnes de Grace consoled, "Lose some, win some."

While casting his eyes about to match the cast-about in his mind for something clever/romantic/suggestive to say using the word *winsome,* though he wasn't sure he would say it anyway, Apple saw a familiar Rolls-Royce convertible. It was parked in the kerb, anti-thief device posed elegantly on the white down-folded top.

Extra pleased with himself for the way he was keeping alert whatever the circumstances, Apple was able to edge a lordliness into his, "You may drop me here, Aggers."

"We're not there yet."

"I'll jog a block or two."

Bringing the car to a stop: "Just so long as we don't exhaust ourselves, darling."

Other innuendo from both sides followed, while Apple got out, and ended with the blonde's, "See you out front after the bout, darling." The limousine glided off.

Apple strolled back. He had no plan in mind. But he was full and shining, and therefore felt he couldn't go wrong and indeed could be inclined to go right.

He looked in a coffee shop, a shoe store, a barber's. No Samuel Glacier. He went close enough to the Rolls-Royce to poise a touching finger and get stared at by the guard. He peered around the door of a beer parlour, nodded, went in.

Signs on the walls warned against standing, singing, spitting, gambling. No one was singing in the straggly circle of men standing around the table where Samuel Glacier and others were gambling at poker, though one envious kibitzer looked as if he might spit.

Apple sat at a table nearby, sharing with an old man who kept winking to show he wasn't really on the verge of dozing off. A circulating waiter came and from his tray unloaded a goblet of beer for Apple, who, after paying, exchanged it discreetly for the old man's empty glass.

The poker game went on. Each pot held several hundred dollars. Nobody seemed to be getting any pleasure from the play. Losers gave sardonic smiles, winners frowned, audience sighed. Apple waited to be blessed with an idea.

His table companion discovered the beer, believed it when he tasted it, and went on tasting until the glass was empty. The game continued, with Samuel Glacier having more than his share of wins.

It was when the old man had made two more discoveries, was beginning to hum on free beer, that his secret benefactor saw what he could do. The answer had been there on a distant table all along: a pack of cards.

Apple got up and made his way to the washroom, where he passed time by avoiding graffiti. Returning, he circled to the far table. There he sat long enough to separate an ace from the pack, held down out of sight. This he palmed as he slowly moved in on the circle of watchers around the poker game.

Once there he didn't pause. With a clear, "You dropped something," he stepped to Samuel Glacier's side. He stooped and rose again, apparently bringing up the card, which he made sure was seen around as an ace. "Yours."

The gambler shrugged, seeming unconcerned. "Not mine."

Worriedly Apple looked around the assembly. No one was impressed. A player said an irritated, "Deal, deal." Another told Apple, "Move your ass."

He protested, "But this ace was under this gentleman's chair. He must've dropped it."

Bored, Samuel Glacier tapped the back of his cards. "Wrong pack, fella."

Looking down, Apple saw that his ace had a back of blue flowers, whereas the game pack had pink dots. He said, "Oh."

For the first time the professional gambler glanced up at Apple's face. He did a stylish double-take and a crinkle came across his brow.

Quietly he said, "Hey."

As a diverter, Apple flicked the card away, doing so with ample body language. Everybody looked at the card's flight, including Samuel Glacier. Apple slipped away feeling slightly less moronic than he deserved.

He got the idea while he was taking a shower, which followed a late nap. Between came a telephone call from the Festival's bout coordinator. He informed that Silver Flash would be third on the bill tonight, after the Bull Massive match.

So, with one of his marks in mind, he gazed across the bathroom at the bottles and jars he had been supplied with by Upstairs to aid his act of being in a bruise-prone profession. It was then that Apple came up with the idea which had been loitering since he had seen names on the marquee.

Details he worked on while getting dry and donning an appearance-changer: a tracksuit in bright blue. He ran through the whole campaign on his drive downtown.

You score some drug that's illegal in athletics; you contrive to get Bull Massive to ingest same; after his bout you demand that he submit to a urine test; it, of course, proves positive; the famous wrestler is shot down in the flames of disgrace; the Trio is reduced to a Duo.

Humming, Apple drove slowly the whole length of Emperor Avenue and started back again, slowly still. He kept an acute eye out on either side. He was not worried by failing so far to spot the man he wanted. If

Knotty wasn't available he could always go to the same source as before, but he could do without Chuck's cute remarks on where all these drugs were going. Besides, Knotty probably dealt in a better class of merchandise.

Again Apple turned at a dwindling of the main thoroughfare's businesses, and started back. As he crawled along, he began to feel the first scrapings of guilt. He let them increase, grow to rasps, though he did shake his head in denial. He had long since stopped humming.

When the rasps turned to gashes Apple defended that he was not fully to blame. If the old boy went home sozzled after his free beers and got into trouble with his wife it was his own fault.

The defence was so logical, so fair, that Apple was in danger of losing this guilt, which would leave him open to another. Therefore he derided his naiveté. Of course he was partly at fault for the old sot being drunk, staggering home in loutish mood to his long-suffering wife . . .

Knotty. Apple saw him ahead. He was leaning against a store window as though about to ask passers-by if they had been saved. Apple looked for a parking space, saw none, decided not to double and drove on. Around the first corner he found a slot at once. He parked and hurried back.

"Yes," Knotty said by way of greeting.

Apple said, "Hi. We've met before."

"Sure we have. I never forget a face. Can't afford to in my line of work."

"Absolutely."

"You play basketball with the Windsor Wings, right?"

"Right."

"I gotta gift for it, the memory stuff."

"How lucky you are."

"True," Knotty said. "See, if I ever get questioned by the fuzz, which does happen despite them usually dismissing me as a nowhere man, I'm able to help 'em out with the straight word on customers."

"Really?"

"Yours, for instance, would be basketballer, dark, olive complexion, name of Percival."

With quiet respect for the dealer's brilliance, Apple said, "Yes, I do see what you mean."

"So what can I do for ya, kid?"

"I want to turn on with something that's truly banned. It's not the junk itself that hits me, it's the knowledge that I'm being real illicit."

"You got all the right instincts, kid," Knotty said. "And it so happens that I have about my person a little number that would turn heads in Marrakesh."

"That sounds the very thing."

Shyly: "It's my own recipe."

"You are a man of many talents."

All business: "You got twenty bucks?"

Some minutes later Apple was walking alone to his car. The exchange, conducted in an alley, had put into his pocket one large green pill.

Apple ate dinner in a suburban restaurant. He made three trips to the salad bar. He declined dessert but had a black coffee because it would be all to the good if he wasn't tired tonight.

Tapping his toe to the Muzak, Apple tried not to feel sorry for his fellow diners, who might never know the limelight. He kept safely alive his simmer of guilt over the old man, and bet four million dollars with himself that before he left here the waitress would ask for his autograph.

He lost. Feeling richer as well as comfortingly cynical—a man you couldn't fool when it came to human nature—he paid and strolled out. A five percent tip, he assured himself, was perfectly in order for indifferent service.

On seeing the tall crew-cutted, bow-tied man approaching from the parking lot, Apple did a fast turn aside and darted to a telephone box. He stayed behind it until Walter Speedy Bane of the *Post* had passed inside the restaurant as though leading an entourage.

He could well do without discussing with Bane the biography of Albert Watkin the plumber. That was one life story which assuredly would never see the light of day.

Driving, Apple scripted, *Naturally enough, over the years agent Porter was often approached by writers who wanted to ghost his memoirs. He refused, unmoved by the considerable sums of money mentioned. Gold had never been his goal. Greed had no home in his soul. He cared only for duty.*

And some people, Apple mused while whistling the theme music from today's movie, didn't even leave five. Some didn't tip at all. So it was perfectly in order.

The changing room held thirty or forty men. Wrestlers, seconds, trainers, managers, hangers-on; they were spread about in groups and singles, with the largest gathering around Bull Massive, who was changing. Already changed was a combatant limbering up for the first bout.

Apple took his carton of orange juice, which he had bought at a drive-in, straight into the washroom. It was deserted. Pulling two paper cups from a dispenser, he filled them with juice and tutted about that old sot.

A man came in. Apple pretended to be examining a pimple in the mirror until he was alone again, when he brought out the green pill. He dropped it into one of the cups, stirred with a finger, felt the pill dissolve.

Being no amateur, Apple allowed, he had no intentions of getting caught by that hackneyed business of getting the drinks mixed. With a thumbnail he put ridges around the rim of one cup in the style of a pie's edge. He worked with concentration and was pleased with the symmetrical result.

His feeling paled once he was back in the changing room. He stood there with a cup in either hand surveying the scene and thinking of his plan. It seemed absurd suddenly, his intention of going to Bull Massive and saying, "It's my birthday. Have a drink with me." Why only Massive and none of the others? Plus other awkwardnesses.

Apple stood, cogitating worriedly. Minutes passed, the first-bout wrestler left. Apple tried:

"I hear you're an orange-juice expert, B.M. Could you give an opinion on this, please?"

"Promotion says this cup can be held without buckling by the strongest of men, so . . ."

"I think that the world's finest wrestler ought to have a taste of the world's finest . . ."

"The one who sinks his drink first . . ."

Unconvinced, and unaware that he had been the focus of puzzled gazes, Apple moved on. He went over to the bench by his locker, on top of which he set the cups. Thinking still, he started to change. He felt confident he would come up with the right angle.

The dressing room had a new centre of attraction.

Big Chief Running Bear, a German-American from New Jersey, stepped out into a pacifistic war dance. He wanted, he had announced, to see if his new headdress would hold up in action. The performance was helped along by the audience's appreciative hoots, laughter and applause. Apple sniffed his envy of the dancer's nerve.

By the time Big Chief Running Bear had given up, breathless, Apple had changed into his wrestling gear and cape. Forgetfully, he had even put on his mask. Reaching for the rear zip to unhood again (there would be a long wait before his bout), he held when he saw coming toward him none other than Bull Massive himself. The wrestler was carrying a bottle of champagne and a plastic mug.

"There you are," he said. "Have a drink with me, S.F."

"A drink?"

"It's my wedding anniversary."

"Well, I don't know."

"Come on, S.F., a sip won't hurt you. We're all having a wee drop. Just a token."

"Of course. Great idea."

Bull Massive handed over the mug. "Knock it back."

Apple, who had no intentions of drinking, as he disliked champagne, was involved with making two plans at the same time. The first he got on the road at once, saying with a tip of his head, "That's hilarious."

When Bull Massive turned back to him from having followed the direction of his nod and gaze, Apple was holding to his mouth the plastic mug, which he had emptied onto the shoulder of his cape—a splash on a hard surface could be heard, as he knew from Training Six.

"What's hilarious?" Bull Massive asked.

Apple played deaf. With a smack of his lips he put the inverted mug on top of Massive's bottle. "Delicious, B.M.," he said. "And now you must have a drink with me. Today is my birthday. Okay?"

"Sure thing, S.F."

"I'm afraid I only have orange juice, but at least it's good and healthy."

"Juice is just dandy with me."

Apple turned to the locker, reached for the cups. There he paused. The rim ridges stood out clearly, but he couldn't remember if they were to mark the drugged drink or the clean one.

Bull Massive asked, "Well?"

Apple picked up the cups and turned. One he veered toward the wrestler, brought it back; he semi-offered the other, snapped it away; he held out the first again, changed his mind; he nearly succeeded in getting the other across.

With his free hand going forward and back, Bull Massive asked, "What's the problem?"

"The problem is, B.M., I can't recall which of these two I cut with water," Apple said. "I'd hate like hell to give you watered orange juice."

"Oh, I don't care. Gimme that one."

"No no."

"Okay, that one."

"No," Apple said, sweating. He wondered how much of his loss of memory was the work of his conscience.

Bull Massive said, "Heck, S.F., now you got me hot for juice. Any cup'll do."

"Congratulations on your wedding anniversary."

"Thanks. And a happy birthday to you. Why don't I just drink them both?"

Apple put the cups behind his back. "Watered orange juice is notoriously bad for the system."

"Are you kidding?"

A bell rang. It signalled the end of the first bout. At once Bull Massive lost interest both in the orange juice and its doubtful purveyor. Swinging around, he went at a jog over to his place. Apple sat on the bench weakly.

Dull, he watched the first-match wrestler come in, grinning from his victory, watched Bull Massive leave in a swirl of people. He told himself he had missed a golden opportunity due to some kind of mental aberration.

Looking down at the cups in his hands, Apple immediately remembered which was the one he ought to have handed over. It, of course, had the pie-edge ridges.

Rising, Apple moved off with the cups. In the washroom he emptied the guilty drink into a basin and swilled it away. The other he drank.

Cups thrown in the wastebasket, Apple returned to his seat on the bench. He looked around. After a while he wondered if he should go to watch the Massive bout.

No, he decided. The right thing to do was sing a song. That was perfectly obvious.

Getting up again, clearing his throat, Apple called out, "Quiet, please! Quiet! Let's have a bit of order! No more talking there! Silence!"

When he stopped, there was not a sound to be heard. Gratified, he launched into a rendering of

"When Our Lucy Came Home Late," a Victorian music hall ballad with sixteen risqué verses. He sang standing at attention. He sang while his eyes roved with appreciation around the men who were attending in total silence and immobility. He sang with feeling.

Ballad over at long last, the audience's coughs and frail claps finished, Apple bowed and went over to a massage table, where he stretched out on his back. Watching the rise and fall of the ceiling (they were so clever in the New World), he planned how he would be a graceful loser.

The referee stepped nimbly aside, the crowd gave throat to its pleasure and excitement, the combatants circled an invisible pole with their hands seeming ready to break a limb, rip off an ear or gouge an eye.

Mad Mountain Phil portrayed the most menace. A big burly man in goatskin trunks, with a face like a deflated punch-bag, he grimaced and glowered as though his cave was about to be taken over by bears.

A voice called, "Don't spare the lash, Flash!"

In glancing crowdward in response, Apple noticed Agnes de Grace. He hadn't done so earlier. He had been too busy with parading around the ring, feeling jealous of that goatskin garment and debating whether or not to treat the crowd to a song or two.

After signalling a friendly hold-everything-be-right-back to his opponent, Apple swung away and went to the ropes. The top one he held while leaning over swayingly to offer salutations to the actress.

Agnes de Grace, in her usual front-row seat, was wearing an electric-blue with its hem up at mid-thigh and neckline down at near-illegal. The greeting she returned with smiles and regal waves.

A blow caught Apple in the ribs. He went blundering sideways and arrived in a corner. Turning, he collected himself in time to receive a kick on the shin from Mad Mountain Phil, which made him laugh.

His opponent snarled, "Oh yeah?"

Falling to all-fours, Apple crawled cheerfully back to opposite the blonde, where, despite the advantageous position he had shrewdly assumed, he still couldn't see up her dress. They exchanged more waves and smiles.

"Get on with the bash, Flash!"

"Let your teeth gnash, Flash!"

"Get into the clash, Flash!"

What they really wanted was a song, Apple decided. He was on the point of getting up when his ankles were grabbed. He was dragged across the ring on his face, flipped over, and then dropped on heavily by his opponent.

Apple thought this quite amusing. He cooperated with the referee by keeping still, shoulders to the canvas, so the man could get cleanly through a count of three.

The crowd roared; the man in goatskin leapt up with a whoop; Apple got to his feet and bowed all around before accepting from Agnes de Grace a blown kiss. The referee bellowed that the first fall had gone to Mad Mountain Phil.

With Apple telling himself he must try to be more involved, the combatants faced each other again. His opponent didn't look particularly old, Apple mused. But he must be if his cousin Agnes had said so; therefore he was bound to know how to get out of a Mangler.

"Let's have some dash, Flash!"

"Turn'm into trash, Flash!"

Other voices called:

"Go for the kill, Phil!"

"Give him the drill, Phil!"

Swiftly, Apple took a one-handed hold which he had learned at Damian House ten years ago. It consisted of arranging the fingers on one of the subject's hands so that if he didn't move as commanded his fingers would break.

The present subject moved.

With his eyes showing their whites in a way Apple thought most effective, Mad Mountain Phil began to circle the gripper, whose arm, like his own, was fully outstretched. At first it was like a dance, especially with the fulcrum humming; then it became more like the in-breaking of a horse, as Apple turned on his heel at a more interesting speed.

Mad Mountain Phil ran, his free arm making feeble grabs at space. The crowd roared.

Apple hummed an ever-bright tune, one that would have been at home on a fairground. He felt as though he were at the centre of a merry-go-round, a private carousel with only a single horse, but one that was a satisfyingly dramatic galloper, wild of eye and foam-flecked of mouth.

"Stir the mash, Flash!"

"Stop the mill, Phil!"

Apple wasn't sure how long he continued the Mangler, whose purpose he had forgotten. He released his hold when he began to feel a slight dizziness. It quickly faded.

Mad Mountain Phil went on running. His inside arm was still sticking out. With knees lifting, he looked like a direction-signalling cyclist who had forgotten his bike.

Apple applauded.

Gradually slowing, gasping, giving a sad smile, Mad Mountain Phil came to a sagged halt. He then fell over onto his back, as void of bounce as a dirge.

Apple stepped close. He stooped, placed his hands in friendly fashion on Mad Mountain Phil's shoulders and asked, "We're not going to sleep, are we?"

The referee came, crouched, pounded canvas and shouted, "One! Two! Three!" As he got up he drew Apple erect with him, adding, "Second fall to Silver Flash!"

The crowd stood to cheer.

Apple paraded. He bowed. He preened. He blew kisses from alternate palms. He tried to remember if he had already sung to his fans or was due to.

Into his vision clicked Agnes de Grace. Apple went over and looked down. Deciding on subtlety instead of that blatant peering, he called:

"What's the colour of your drawers, Aggers?"

The actress, her smile less full than before, answered by staring up at him in a meaningful way, which Apple chose to take as meaning he had committed a gaffe. Perhaps, he reasoned, one did not ask ladies questions of that nature.

Hands around his mouth, Apple shouted down, "Sorry about that."

Agnes de Grace's lips formed, "It would be nice if it did not happen again."

"Don't worry, it won't."

Her smile came on full.

At a call from the referee Apple turned away. By way of atonement, he thought, he would do his best to make her cousin look good. This was, after all, one of the man's last bouts in a long career.

After a spell of the pair stalking each other, while the crowd called for mayhem and manslaughter, Mad Mountain Phil rushed in and secured a bear-hug. He heaved upward. Apple was lifted off his feet.

But how trite, he thought in disdain. Was this the way to conclude a distinguished career in the ring? Was this something to tell your grandchildren? Was this a paragraph you wanted in your biography?

Even while wondering what lock or grapple to use in putting an end to the situation, Apple automatically reached down to his opponent's ribs: tickling, the world's oldest form of disablement.

Apple tickled.

With a high-pitched shriek like schoolgirl hysteria, the wrestler let his load drop. He stepped back. His features twitched as they shifted between a grin and a leer and a murderous frown.

He growled, "Watcha think you're doing?"

"Helping," Apple said.

Snapping forward, he took a two-handed grip on his opponent's arm. It was another oldie, standard in espionage's dirty fighting but largely unknown to people who attacked one another for reasons personal (as opposed to political; the first being illegal but the second having the blessings of all governments).

The pressure placed by the grip on pulse, ligaments, muscle and funny bone combined to deliver a sensation like an electric shock.

Apple pressed.

With a yelp Mad Mountain Phil leapt into the air, sideways, like a dancer clicking his heels. Coming down hard, he landed shakily on bent legs.

The crowd ranted approval.

"That's more like the stuff," Apple said encouragingly. "You looked really wild." He still held the grip.

"Listen," the wrestler gasped.

"Off you go."

"Look—"

Apple applied pressure again, and again Mad Mountain Phil, face agape, performed his leap. He descended with a loud, ring-dithering thud.

"Great," Apple told him before sending him up once more.

"Put'm on the grill, Phil!"

"Turn him into ash, Flash!"

The up-down, up-down continued, until a strange expression on the wrestler's face caused Apple to wonder if this sort of activity might not be all that good for his rheumatism. He released the grip.

Quickly, before Mad Mountain Phil could sink to the canvas, which he seemed inclined to, Apple turned and reached behind to take him by the wrists. He forced the hands onto his own neck so it would look as if he was being strangled from the rear by the blundering wrestler.

Holding the reluctant grip in place with a KGB nerve-lock, wearing a face of worry and discomfort, Apple moved forward. He began to circle the ring, gathering speed and dragging in his wake the stumbling Mad Mountain Phil, who, Apple assured himself, would appear to be victoriously chasing his chicken opponent.

Soon they were running. The crowd bellowed like race-goers when the horses come into the straight. The referee, a veteran, kept well out of the way.

"Cut off the dash, Flash!"

"Where there's a will, Phil!"

Apple felt fine and fit; felt he could go on running forever. Progress, however, presently became more difficult because of the brake created by the other man's stumbles and swerves, which were accompanied by groans.

Stopping, Apple let go.

Mad Mountain stood in a heap panting for several seconds before he began to fall forward like a shot lumberjack. He landed on his face with a crash.

Apple knelt beside him. Seeking to help, he rolled him over onto his back. The reason he leaned on him was so he could veer close, be recogniseable to this wrestler with poor vision when he asked, "You okay?"

The answer croaked out by Mad Mountain Phil was lost on Apple because of—in addition to the uproar—the referee's shouted counting.

The rest was confusion. Apple, the victor, gazed around as his arm was raised. He looked at the hats thrown up, dodged thrown roses that got as far as the ring, smiled on the groggily-rising Mad Mountain Phil.

Arm released, Apple felt the confusion happily continue. His head was full of trumpet music and cheering, his eyes were absorbing the action, his hand was frisky with the kisses he was blowing to the crowd. His legs were busy with the business of taking him around so he could give every section of the audience a fair view of him.

Sincerely thanking the referee for herding him into the corner where the steps were, Apple climbed through the ropes and got down. Six people helped him on with his silver cape.

Conditions were more tranquil when Apple reached the changing room, after getting away from two reporters and a television man who thrust a microphone into his face. So tranquil were conditions that, following his shower—during which he declined to sing, because that was what five hundred million people did—he treated the men still present, a dozen or so, to a bowdlerised version of "The Way To A Woman's Heart."

Finished, Apple personally thanked each of the remaining three people for their applause, then started to get out of his wrestling gear. It seemed to take much longer than normal; the shoelaces particularly were obtuse.

Changed at last, Apple wished everyone a sincere, heartfelt good night, twice, left the room and went to the stage door, where its guardian told him, "Lotsa fans out there, S.F." He said it to warn, not to cheer.

Although tempted to go out and please them with a song or several, Apple thought of Agnes de Grace. He didn't want to keep her waiting. He made his way to the front of the building.

Out on the street Apple was surprised to see no limousine standing in the curb. But he quickly realised that—as the date wasn't really here, it was for supper at the house—Aggers would have gone there after his match and be expecting him to do that same thing.

He went to get his car. Nothing happened on the way, which seemed wrong to him. He glared all around petulantly, and even waited a while before unlocking the rented Ford.

Driving, Apple started to feel slightly peculiar. It wasn't unpleasant, just different. Repeatedly he got a sinking sensation, as though he were an elevator descending, following which he shuddered from hair to toenails.

Externals too had changed. There was less prettiness about the lights—those of the downtown area and of the vehicles that zipped around him dangerously.

When all lights had gone except his own car's, when he was out on a country road, Apple of a sudden asked, aloud, "Did I really sing?"

Cogitating, he was forced to admit that sing he had, more than once. He had stood boldly there in the changing room and blasted away like Caruso.

That he didn't blush at the memory of making a fool of himself might have caused Apple to be embarrassed at his coarseness—if it hadn't been that he felt thrilled.

Could this, he wondered, mean that he was losing his shyness? Could he be developing an outgoing personality? Or, more sinister (and more thrilling), was the glamour of being a big star in the professional wrestling firmament going to his head, so that he was growing a hard shell?

Apple was still enjoying these questions when he turned through a gateway set in a stretch of white fencing. A track took him to a windbreak of tall trees, beyond which he came in sight of Agnes de Grace's temporary home.

It was turn of the century, a three-story frame house with turrets and ornate fixtures, and a wrap-around porch with latticework. Painted white, it looked as though it belonged in a horror comic. Some of the lower windows showed mellow light and a lamp hung over the door.

Apple parked by the front steps. On getting out, aware of the cricket-scratched silence, he recalled another point relating to his big-star glamour: tonight he had won the match when it would have been better both privately and professionally if he had lost.

Angus Watkin would not like the high profile, Apple knew, and Aggers might tease him about taking advantage of an older, rheumatic, near-retiree with poor eyesight.

In order to give a world-weary sigh, with which he would slowly shake his head, Apple took in a deep breath. At once he got an up-elevator sensation. Grinning, he told himself that if it were true what fame was doing to his personality—okay. Reality had quite a different aspect. Sometimes.

Apple went up the steps to the porch. Treading softly on boards, he ignored the main door and moved to the nearest glowing window. He listened. From behind the drapes there was only the burble of a television set to be heard. He went on toward the next window.

When he asked himself why he was sneaking around like a thief, Apple received the astounding, thrilling reply that famous and powerful people had rights that lesser mortals lacked. His eyes grew moist at the accompanying notion that he could be turning into a monster.

Apple listened by the heavily curtained window. He could hear voices. There were three, one female and two male. The woman he recognised as Agnes de Grace. The other two speakers sounded familiar but he couldn't put name to timbre, even though the more he listened the more convinced he became that he had heard these men before.

Giving up on identity, Apple concentrated on matter, pressing an ear on the glass. But only an occasional word was distinguishable from the flow. The conversation's tone seemed sometimes urgent, sometimes acrimonious, sometimes soothing.

Backing off softly, revelling in the spook-work, Apple went to the front door. He rang a buzzer. Response came fast. The door was opened by a uniformed maid.

Smiling, she said, "Good evening, sir." Apple had heard her voice before, on the telephone.

"Good evening, young lady," he said, bowing. "An admirer to see Ms. de Grace."

"I'll see if she's home."

"She is."

The maid tilted her head. She had dimples in her chin, her cheeks and on her brow. She asked, "How d'you know?"

"A little voice told me."

Winking: "Hold the fort." She closed the door.

Apple hummed until the maid returned, when he ended his tune in a dirge key. The smile had disappeared, and the dimples had gone. She said, "Madame is not at home and in any case she's sick to death of secret admirers. Good night."

Apple stopped the door from closing fully. "She doesn't know which secret admirer I am."

"How can she if she's not here?"

He could, Apple supposed, have been wrong about hearing Aggers. He asked, "If she's not at home, where could she be?"

"Maybe the reception. Who knows? I only empty ashtrays in this place."

"The reception at the Crown?"

"I dunno. What you should do is ask your little voice. And so good night."

Turning from the closed door, Apple went down the

steps. He wondered if possibly the actress was avoiding him—if, in fine, she had taken a deeper offence than he had assumed.

Yes, Apple thought, getting in the car, a lady of Aggers' sensitive nature could very well be offended by being asked what colour her drawers were. Maybe claiming certain rights didn't work out so well after all.

He drove off, heading for town, and for the reception.

FOUR

Receptions and parties relating to the Festival had been happening right along, as Apple well knew, since his mailbox at the Puck Motel was always clogged with invitations. Such affairs he had avoided like thick-sole shoes; they would be no help at all in his attempt at maintaining a dwarf profile in Empire, Ontario.

But did that matter at this stage of the caper?—Apple asked of himself as he parked the car on a side street. Did anything at all matter? He got out and locked up. Did it matter if anything mattered or didn't matter? He walked away shaking his head.

Apple felt a different sort of odd from his earlier oddness, he discovered. He didn't feel bad, he didn't feel good. He had a kind of apprehensive confidence.

Weighing emotions, Apple decided his condition was like being that elevator when it was stuck between floors. You were sure you would soon get up or down, but were worried that, ceasing to believe this, you would panic.

After a two-block walk Apple came to the Crown, one of the major hotels. It boasted a doorman, who closed one cold eye at Apple, who approached in a lean. Apple winked back.

Inside the lobby, he had no need to ask for directions or look for arrows. A loud rumble led him to a corner and along a corridor and around a corner—and into the action, which, evidently, had already hit its peak and was now in the process of untidily declining.

The room, as cramped as half a football field, had a long table stretching down either side. One table was for food, the other for drinks; both were now in a state that would have appealed only to vultures. Between the two disasters heaved the crowd, particles of which were leaving.

Feeling boldly insecure, Apple ventured into the throng to look for Agnes de Grace so he could jog her memory about their intimate little supper.

What he found straight away was Batter Brown, whom he told a cheery, "Greetings, B.B."

The short, fat and hairy wrestler stared aggressively. He asked a slipshod, "Who inell're you?"

"I'm Silver Flash."

The aggression hid behind a smirk. "Well well well. I wondered when I was going to run into you."

"Right, B.B."

"Pity I'm not in my car."

Apple obliged with a chuckle. "I must remember that one. I really must. Really."

"And while you're struggling to do that," Batter Brown said, "we'll have a nice talk about how you got me to foul you."

"You're quite mistaken, B.B."

"Why not just call me an idiot?"

"Is that a genuine query?" Apple asked sincerely.

He backed off against other people, not wishing to become embroiled in a serious discussion.

"Are you a genuine jerk?"

"If so, we'll take it up some other time, B.B. I have a date. So long."

"Hold it, Silver Trash," Batter Brown snarled through his smirk. He reached out a grab hand.

Apple avoided it so neatly that he laughed, which caused people to separate, which enabled him to slip away. He laughed again. Several people laughed back at him, knowingly.

After progressing some metres through the throng Apple looked behind. He saw that the wrestler was coming, determination steely in his eyes.

Musing that he did like people with a sense of humour, while at the same time warning himself that Batty Brown wasn't kidding, Apple forged on.

"Pity I'm not in my car," he told a woman whose path he crossed. She stared at him blankly. He went on with a forgiving and pitying smile.

"Why, if it's not—um—you."

"Good evening, S.F."

Speedy Bane's bow-tie moved up and down as though he had pressed a button. "Here you are. The plumber with the human interest story to sell."

"Seen Aggers around?"

"Who?"

"Agnes de Grace. Seen her anywhere?"

With his bow-tie jiggling, the reporter said, "She must be a friend of yours."

"No. And forget the life story. Too many people would be hurt."

"You mean celebrities? Names? The Beautiful Persons and the Jet Setters?"

To his own imitation annoyance Apple offered one of those I-refuse-to-divulge smiles, the kind used by gossips to mask their pain when they realise they are going to be the last to know. He said:

"The life story idea is out."

Speedy Bane flicked his eyes from side to side, asking, "Have we, perhaps, been warned? Threatened?"

"We have not."

"Omerta?"

Apple, who had only slowed to a shuffle, not stopped, quickened his pace. "Ask me no questions . . ." he said. "You know the rest of it. Must go."

The reporter said, "Wait wait, wait wait."

"That's Batty Brown coming this way."

"Seen him a million times."

"He just won the federal lottery."

"He just won—?"

Apple ploughed on. Looking back a moment later he saw the wrestler being intercepted by Speedy Bane. Both were thrumming with determination.

Turning away, smug with his brilliance, Apple sank at the knees to handle the next skirmish through the crowd; when free, he straightened in order to scan about, and continued with this switch as he circulated.

He stepped on an old man's toes, swung back to apologise and stepped on the other foot. "No," he snapped at a woman who asked him if he was Gorgeous Gordon. He floundered on.

"What's your hurry, string bean?"

The question came from Tiny Bomb. He timed it with a clamp on Apple's wrist. "We mustn't go charging around like a freaky lamp-post, must we?"

Apple, held, said, "Expecting a phone call."

"I know you, seems to me."

"I just hit town."

"Seems to me there's only one freckled nose around like that. Right, Silver Flash?"

"That's not my name."

The wrestler said, "Don't worry, Tiny Bomb's not really mine. But we won't tell anyone, eh?"

"Excuse me, I have to go."

"I'll go with you. We can have a peaceful chat about that deliberate head-butt of yours."

"It was quite innocent."

"I been to your motel several times. You're never there. But now I got lucky. Come on."

"You have no idea how innocent it was," Apple protested as he reached for the other man's elbow.

Increasing his wrist-clasp, Tiny Bomb said, "We'll go to the back alley, I think. Alleys make the best places for chats about—" He turned into a statue as the pinched nerve sizzled a warning in his head.

Like stealing a candy kiss from a baby, Apple took his wrist out of the wrestler's clasp. He moved well back in a stoop, and stretched out his arm before releasing the suffering elbow. He slipped away.

A grinning man with two full glasses paused in midlurch to offer one of them to Apple, who neatly put the grinner behind him as a smidgen of rearguard action.

Uncheered, Apple wondered if he should get the hell out of here and go home. But what if Aggers was around somewhere, looking for him while he was looking for her? What if she was wringing her hands?

Apple tried to conjure up a picture of the actress wringing her hands as she struggled through the mob. Nothing came. Giving up, he told himself he couldn't leave yet because if she were here she would feel stood up, which, on top of being asked in public about the shade of her drawers, might tend to make her less enthusiastic about him than before.

The uproar of talk was pierced locally by a laugh, which sounded like the lilt produced by Agnes de Grace. In changing directions, Apple glanced behind.

Struggling after him through the crowd, one behind the other, were Batter Brown, Speedy Bane and Tiny Bomb.

That laugh belonged to a hearty matron, one who withered into a state of anxiety when Apple glared at her in loathing and accusation.

He went on.

He almost ran into the territory of John Bark, the tall, pimply, pale, buck-toothed, balding English fan. At the last second Apple shrank, swerved, scooted low past a dozen people, circled a pillar, stopped at last and stood up to his normal height.

He was face to face with Mad Mountain Phil, who said, like a stone, "Good-bye."

"Hello there, M.M.P."

"Good-bye."

"I'm Silver Flash."

"So someone just told me. Good-bye."

"Things didn't work out quite the way I expected tonight," Apple said. "I don't know why."

"Nor me," the wrestler grunted. He did a military about-face and moved off.

Apple followed. "Where you going?"

"To get away from you."

"Why's that, M.M.P.?"

"I don't wanna break your leg."

"Course not."

"I'd get the jail."

Apple said, "I know it must be a bitter disappointment to you, not being able to end your career as a winner."

Cast back: "End my career? What you babbling about?"

"Retirement. Because of your age. Not that you look it. I dare say you've had a bit of plastic surgery done, a few tucks here and there."

"Christ, now it's insulting me," Mad Mountain Phil said. "I'm years away from retiring and I'll be thirty next birthday. I gotta get away from this."

Guilty, Apple persisted, "And it can't be easy for you, not with that awful rheumatism of yours."

"Never had rheumatism in my life, you jerk. I'm the fittest man in this town."

"I know how it is. We try to hide these things. Particularly if they interfere with our professions."

"Christ. Stop following me."

Apple said with sympathy, "And then there's your vision. You can hardly see a thing. Age, I suppose. Have you thought of trying contact lenses?"

Abruptly, Mad Mountain Phil stopped and turned. "Okay," he said in resignation. "I get the jail."

"What's up?"

"Both legs."

"You misunderstand, M.M.P. I'm not insulting you. I happen to have learned of your infirmities from your cousin."

"What cousin?"

Apple said, "Aggers."

"Who the fluke is Aggers?"

"Why, Agnes de Grace, naturally."

Mad Mountain Phil glared. He was quivering. He

said in a lethal quietness, "She ain't no cousin of mine, nerd, bastard, creep. The women in my family either marry and have ten kids or they become missionaries."

Alarmed that the man might explode, Apple backed off. At the same time, he looked behind and saw that Batter Brown, Tiny Bomb and Speedy Bane were getting closer. He decided to call it a day—if he were free to do so.

"We'll take this up some other time," he said.

Mad Mountain Phil was flexing fingers. "The time is now."

Suddenly Apple shot down to a squat. In this position he waddle-walked through the forest of people and reached the nearest long table. Crawling beneath it, he went on all-fours toward the exit. In spirit he was even lower. The elevator had sunk to the garbage area.

Apple awoke to the chirping of aches. They were all over him, but especially in his legs, which, he found, he was unable to straighten from their acute angle.

He thought about it.

The best theory, that he had stayed under the table on all-fours, lasted until he finally gathered together enough courage to open his eyes. He saw he was in a car.

His own rented Ford, he was curled up in its back as naturally as a hibernating giraffe. He remembered now having made it to the car and then feeling too wrecked to make any further moves.

Ten painful minutes Apple spent in extricating himself from the Ford and in wobbling through calisthenics. His chirps slowly faded, he stopped wanting to groan, and the children who had formed a fascinated audience continued on their way to school, uplifted.

Apple set off along the residential street. In mind and body he gradually improved. It was a clear, keen, sunny morning and he was feeling pleasantly jaded.

Which, he reminded himself, he had every right to feel. He had been out on the razzle, you might say, and he had slept rough. He needed a shave, his hair was a mess, his clothing was rumpled and creased. No doubt he looked like hell. Looked, in fact, like a hell-rake, a man who was no stranger to the seamier side of life, to sleazy dives, to women of easy virtue and particularly to strong booze.

That he had drunk nothing alcoholic yesterday Apple shied away from; otherwise he would have to face up to the suspicion that he had been drugged, which he would not at all have minded if it weren't for the fact that he had made an embarrassing mistake: that he had thrown away the innocent orange juice and imbibed the spiked one.

Apple let the whole ridiculous thing go as he came abreast of a corner grocery store. On the front page of the newspaper in the outside dispenser was a photograph of Silver Flash, caught blowing a kiss.

Apple observed the dispenser from several angles while patting himself for coins. Walking on again after his purchase, he assured himself there was no reason to feel uncomfortable about buying two copies of the edition. Press coverage was all a part of show business, and there were possible grandchildren to think about.

Apple pictured himself standing by a hearth, white of head and handsome. Around his feet play assorted children who have small voices and no noisy toys. Apple lingered over the scene for a full minute, taken particularly by the old man's excessive age shrinkage, before turning to the press.

The story to match the photograph was in the sports pages. It spoke of the hooded wrestler's brilliant if unorthodox win over Mad Mountain Phil, his emergence as one of the Festival's more colourful figures, the oddness that he seemed unknown to British wrestling circles.

In a piece on another page a columnist mused about the possibility of Silver Flash being not from Britain but right here on the doorstep—a local boy trying to make good. The piece closed with, "Maybe S.F. will fess up tonight, take off his mask when, not if, he loses to Eskimo Mel, who, for this writer's money, is going to win the crown."

Apple read that final sentence aloud in case his chief, Angus Watkin, could hear, in some weird paranormal way. He would be pleased to learn that his underling's high profile wasn't going to last for ever.

Apple had breakfast in a suburban eatery which, he believed, he had been in before. Chastened by the columnist's opinion, he sat on his newspapers. He even left one of them behind afterward, when he went to pay his check and give a fifteen percent tip.

On the walk back to his car, Apple changed sides of the street more than once in order to see his jaded reflection in store windows.

He drove off. He wouldn't have minded betting that those people who glanced his way could tell at once that here was a man who had been out on the tiles; a man who hob-nobbed with movie stars and got his picture on the front pages of the world's newspapers. He left it there before he went too far.

Parking at the Puck Motel, Apple went into the office. Only partly was he aware of stifling a yawn and of rubbing a hand across his stubble. The girl at the desk told him that several people had been looking for him yesterday and would probably be back this morning.

Apple went quickly up to his unit. While showering he recalled his meeting last night with Mad Mountain Phil. He didn't blame the wrestler for denying his age and infirmities, but couldn't understand why he pretended not to be related to the delightful Agnes de Grace.

Apple tried to resolve the question of the blonde's non-appearance while changing into jeans and a sweater. He dialled the rented house and got the maid. She said before clicking off, "This phone never works until noon."

Stopping Apple from getting into the peculiarities of some people's servants was an idea, one relating to the mission. He mulled it over as he finished getting ready, shaved, checked through the window for a clear coast below, went down fast to his car and drove off. That he had lost his jaded appearance along with his stubble was, he knew, of no consequence whatever. Apple gently put aside his idea, which was for the destruction of Bull Massive's reputation, when he saw Samuel Glacier. The gambler was strolling along Emperor Avenue as if he had just won it on the turn of a card and was thinking of going for double or nothing.

Since he happened to be heading in the same direction, Apple followed, slowing to a creep and staying well back. When an angled parking slot appeared he steered into it, got out, locked up, and continued tailing on foot.

He whistled and afted his hands to present a picture

of innocence. Occasionally he scratched himself. More usefully, he remembered to keep from looking too long at his mark, for marks were wont to sense a prolonged gaze.

One hour later, when Samuel Glacier went into yet another establishment, (after coffee shop, haberdasher, drug store, florist) Apple was on the verge of admitting to being bored, which would be preferable to facing the fact that he didn't know what he thought he was playing at.

Boldly, after another ten minutes, he ventured closer to the doorway into which Glacier had gone. He then saw that it belonged, signs said, to a pool room.

Entering, Apple went cautiously up stone steps. At the top were swing doors and a smell of dead oxygen. Peeking between the doors he saw a score of billiard tables, all in action. While each had spectators as well as players, most people were gathered around a table at the back.

Footfalls at the bottom of the stairs sent Apple inside, where it was helpfully gloomy apart from the bright slabs of light between green baize and hovering lamp. Another brightness hung over the milk-bar counter.

Circulating slowly and inconspicuously, Apple wasn't surprised, on getting close to the well-attended table, that one of its two players at the game of snooker was Samuel Glacier. By the murmur of talk from the watchers, which paused during shots, and by the studied casualness of the shooters, it was clear that real money was riding on the game.

What was also clear, Apple noted with interest, was that two or three of the spectators were obviously newspapermen. He thought about that as he retreated to the counter and during the drinking of a root beer.

However, no ploy occurred to Apple until he saw a player at a nearby table go to the wall-hung scoreboard and slide his marker along.

Apple returned to the money game.

He spent several minutes among the crowd, working his way around to wall and scoreboard. If anyone glanced at him it was without enough interest for glance to become look, and his head was too far above the light's penumbra for his face to be seen with clarity.

Samuel Glacier's opponent was by far the better player (Apple gathered from talk that he had agreed to a handicap). He was doing most of the scoring. But presently Samuel Glacier got a turn to shoot. He potted two balls, scoring seven points. With Apple looking the other way, he came to the scoreboard, slid the marker along seven notches, and moved on.

Apple already had the coin ready. From a hand poised behind his head, he flipped it far away. Everyone looked around at the clatter of landing, and Apple added another five points to Glacier's score.

When people were turning back, none the wiser about that clatter, Apple was moving to another section of the spectator circle. Once there, he waited.

Nobody noticed the scoreboard.

The other player took his shot, but missed, and Samuel Glacier also failed to score. Apple judged sourly that neither man had much skill. The game went on.

Nobody noticed.

"Say, know what, that there board's been given too many points for Mr. Glacier."

The voice was husky and garrulous and carrying, and it came, Apple was unastonished to realise, from himself. He was quick, having spoken, to duck behind another man.

Respectful silence over, people started agreeing, while craning to see the scoreboard, that the score was too much. Samuel Glacier, appearing bemused, protested that he had added only seven.

Apple smiled. As a smile it wasn't all that rich, and as the seconds passed it became progressively poorer, finally turning needy.

He couldn't bear to witness the framed man's discomfort, Apple discovered; or, he allowed, he couldn't bear to think of it as his own doing.

Either painful way, he had to leave. He slid off, heading for the door. He had just reached it when he heard one of the spectators say, "Wait a bit. There was a tall guy standing over there."

Samuel Glacier said, "Oh?"

After walking briskly around several blocks, Apple went into the bowling alley, where he reluctantly entered its dark telephone box. Dialling a series of numbers, he got connected with a female duty officer.

She asked, "How's everything going, One?"

"Very well."

"That's good. But I'm not deaf, y'know. You don't have to shout."

Needing to keep the door open to appease his claustrophobia, which was heightened by the gloom, Apple had been competing against background racket. "Sorry," he whispered.

"How can we be of service?"

"I want an immediate meeting with Chuck," Apple

said, being super-crisp to counter the woman's casual style, which grated on his romantic view of espionage. "Same place as before."

"No dope?"

"Over and out."

The second call was to Agnes de Grace's house. The maid agreed with Apple that the telephone seemed to be working now. "But if you want Her Highness—too bad. She left to go to a beauty parlour five minutes ago."

At the counter Apple got served with a cheeseburger and milk, which he took to a table. He was glad to have the matter of Agnes de Grace to fret over. It kept him from admitting his relief that his score-cheating ploy in the pool room had probably failed, which abnegated the need for chagrin, which he didn't enjoy all that well.

Apple had finished lunching when a voice at his elbow said, "Boo." He had been expecting something of this light-hearted nature to happen, but since from experience he knew that whatever did happen it was never the expected, Apple twitched with shock.

In recovery, he turned with a raddled smile. "How was that for simulated surprise?"

"First rate, One," Chuck said. He sat, blond and suntanned, yachting cap pushed back on his head. "What can your genie do for you today?"

Trying not to feel jealous of the smart dialogue, Apple said, "I want a woman. Beautiful, alluring, sexy. Above all, a woman who's experienced in feminine wiles."

"Join the club."

"And she'll have to be willing to go through the act of sexual intercourse with a virtual stranger."

"Ask a cabbie or a bellhop, One."

"You're joking, of course."

"Well, I didn't really think you were looking for commercial love, I'll admit."

"I'm looking for an operative who knows the entrapment ropes. A girl who will pick up my mark and waste no time about getting him into bed."

"For purposes of blackmail?"

Worldly, as if he did this sort of thing often, Apple said, "Not at all, Chuck. As a preliminary to having them caught that way."

"And shatter Bull Massive's rep as a faithful husband."

"Now you're cooking with gas," Apple tried. He clenched his toes when Chuck said, grinning, how much he loved hearing these old-fashioned expressions.

"Thought you might enjoy that one."

"So. Where and when do you want the lady?"

"I'll let you know. I had to find out first if such agents were available."

"If they are in Jolly Old, they are here," Chuck said. "You could've asked the duty officer."

Apple stared. "But she's a woman," he said before he could stop himself.

Fortunately, the contact man thought he was hearing a funny line. Apple even joined in the laugh, and he didn't protest more than with a lolled head when Chuck told him he was a real genuine wit.

Apple's armpits had stopped prickling by the time, Chuck having left, he went back to the telephone. With him he took a bar of chocolate, bought at the counter and discarded once he was inside the booth, except for the stiff wrapper, which he balled in one hand and continually squeezed during his call to the Puck.

The crackling thus produced, coupled with what background noise came through the near-closed door, added a touch of authenticity to the endeavour, even though Apple knew that here as in most countries a call from Timbuctoo was liable to have more clarity than one from around the corner. He simply liked feeling that he was being clever.

"Thees ees Roma calling," he told the desk at his motel. "Meester Flavio Mancini wish to speak person-to-person with a Meester Bull Massive."

The girl at the desk, who was usually pretending not to be reading a fashion magazine, started to explain that she had orders that the star wrestler was not to be disturbed. She broke into herself with, "Did you say Flavio Mancini?"

"I deed indid."

"The movie director?"

"Just so."

"Who made *World of Wantons?*"

"That same genius."

"Hold on, Rome," the girl said. "Please."

To avoid dwelling on how close he had come to drawing a blank, Apple continued with his wrapper-crackling and observed his dark reflection in the glass wall. A lip-dangled cigarette, he thought, would be a definite plus.

The receiver came back to life with the voice of Bull Massive. The respect in his tone made it plain that he had been told the identity of the person who was trying to make contact.

"You're through, Mr. Mancini," Apple told himself in Italian. He switched back to English, his broken accent faint, and used another type of voice, for, "Hello, Mr. Massive. Good day. This is Mancini here." Greetings over, he went on, "My personal representative, who arrived in Empire today, has just called me to say he is having difficulties in contacting you."

"Ah yes," the wrestler said. "I can explain that." He told about his need to avoid fans and reporters and other nuisances. "You know how it is."

Soothingly: "But of course."

"Why does your representative wanna contact me, Mr. Mancini?"

"It is connected with a part in a motion picture. I am at present preparing to shoot a modern-dress version of Samson and Delilah. You have no doubt read of my international search for people to play the leads."

"Oh. Yes. Sure. Right."

"You might be perfect for the part of Samson, Mr. Massive. Although, naturally, I would want to fly you here to Rome for a screen test before I could commit myself."

"Why, that's only fair."

"Possibly then you could meet with my representative with no further delay?"

Expansively, Bull Massive said, "I'd be happy to, Mr. Mancini. You just tell me where he's staying."

Chasing that with an extra loud crackle of the wrapper, Apple said, "It is now two-thirty your time. At four o'clock my representative is having a meeting with Eskimo Mel, who is another possible for the Samson rôle."

Cold: "Oh?"

"Perhaps you could make the meeting for three."

"Perhaps I sure as hell could."

"Or for five o'clock, if you wish."

"No no, three's perfect," the wrestler said. "Which is your representative's hotel in Empire?"

Over more heavy crackling Apple said, ". . . and the meeting place is the Colonial Lounge. Probably, Mr. Massive, you are familiar with it."

"Sure," Bull Massive said. "But maybe I'd better check with him first at his hotel."

Loudly over crackling: "Yes, I'm sure you'll get along fine. And don't worry, he'll recognise you. So nice talking to you and hearing you are interested in the part, Mr. Massive. Farewell for the present."

Apple discarded his chocolate wrapper and dialled again. The same female duty officer answered.

Stiffly, Apple said, "The operative discussed with agent Chuck should be in the Colonial Lounge at three o'clock."

The duty officer made a slow tutting sound.

Ignoring that, and what the next person to come in the booth would think on seeing a candy bar by the telephone—all of which made him too busy to need to turn his mind away from the moral aspect of Bull Massive's downfall—Apple left the bowling alley.

Back at the car he wrote:

It is preferable, perhaps, to draw a veil over some of the more sordid aspects of Porter's career. Certainly there were events in Empire that in the years afterward he would never, ever talk about.

Apple clenched his jaw muscles.

The Colonial Lounge, a bar and grill at a thinning end of Emperor Avenue, was imitation Tudor outside and imitation comfortable in. The chairs were too hard and the lighting too harsh. Not that Apple cared.

Sipping ginger-ale, he sat at a table near the wall, whence he had a good view of the whole area. The patrons, twenty or so, were divided between bar and tables. Most now informed each other of the new arrival's identity as Bull Massive came in at a casual lumber.

Before going to sit alone at a table he looked at every person. His glance rested no longer on Apple than on anyone else, evidently fooled, to Apple's relief, by the yachting cap with gold braid, the dark glasses and the false moustache, plus a bulky white track suit that made its wearer appear to be twenty pounds heavier.

While he did have a strong fancy for the goldwork, Apple was proudest of the brush on his top lip. An afterthought in the disguise department, he glimpsed it in passing the novelty shop window. He had been able to dismiss with ease Training Eight's motto that false hairpieces are always a mistake, and the fact that his real hair and the moustache were different shades altogether.

The waiter was leaving, having delivered Bull Massive's soft drink, almost backing off in respect, when another new patron strolled into the lounge.

Apple cringed in doubt.

He could hear in his head a honky-tonk band wailing and hoarse men shouting at her to take it off, take it off, as the girl, not unnoticed by the assembly, sashayed around with belligerent hips.

Her hair was angel blonde, except at the roots, where it was imp black. Her face parodied its own prettiness with a thick layer of cosmetics, like the envious wife of a clown. The shiny scarlet dress was as smooth-fitting as skin, except on the seams, where it puckered in a panic of insecurity.

The girl, whom Apple instantly code-named Stripper, ended her tour at the table of Bull Massive. Leaning down with out-thrust hip, she spoke.

The wrestler listened, shrugged one shoulder, listened, spoke, shook his head, laughed politely, listened, looked at his watch, shrugged again.

Smiling, Stripper sat down.

Apple got up. Unobtrusively he left the lounge. Once outdoors he went at a bustling stride toward the corner of the next block, on which stood a public telephone box.

There was nothing stranger than taste, Apple allowed with a feeling of generosity. One man's fish is another man's fowl. You couldn't argue with the fact that Stripper had quickly got herself on the first rung with Massive, who seemed to be not unattracted. All she had to do was keep it up.

In the box, Apple called the Colonial, asked for the manager, and told him he would be doing Mr. Bull Massive a favour if he gave him a message at once.

"Glad to, glad to."

"Please say that Mr. Mancini's man has been summoned to New York to interview a potential Delilah. He will make contact on his return tomorrow. Thank you."

Apple hurried back to the lounge, and oozed over to his table. Sitting, he relaxed. The wrestler was also looking more at his ease, message obviously received. Now, if he wanted to dally with Stripper, he had the time.

That was the nice thing about this gambit, Apple reckoned—the choice. He told himself how good it was that nobody could blame agent One—especially agent One—if Bull Massive got involved in this business. It was the man's own decision, not like the planting of drugs and such doings. The gambit was almost respectable.

Nevertheless, Apple stayed cheerful as he watched his puppets perform with satisfaction and style, the bald wrestler attentive, Stripper edging her chair closer as she talked, waiter bringing them drinks.

Apple had hardly been aware of the new patron, one of several comers and goers, until she came hesitantly to his table. She held an autograph book.

Stooping, she said, "Excuse me."

Apple played pestered star with a weary, "Yes?"

"Could you please tell me which is Bull Massive?"

"Ahhh," Apple said like a patient with a stick on his tongue, while he rapidly worked out that if he truthfully informed the girl which one the wrestler was, she would interrupt the developing tête-à-tête, maybe disastrously.

He said, "He's not here."

The girl stared at him, which he found a shade unnerving. She was in her early twenties, was conventionally pretty, suited her eye-glasses, wore sweater and straight skirt, and looked as though she ought to be home reading Descartes with a faintly condescending smile.

She asked, "Is that moustache real?"

"Well, no it isn't," Apple said, understanding the stare.

"I didn't think it was."

"We all have our little foibles."

"You're not in disguise?" the girl asked.

"Of course not."

"You wouldn't yourself be Bull Massive, would you?"

"What an idea."

The girl began to straighten, looking around. "Someone told me he was in here."

Hurriedly, Apple said, "Sit down sit down. I do wish people would respect my privacy."

Eagerly the girl said, "I knew it." She sat. "I won't bother you for long, Mr. Massive."

"Call me Bernard."

"Okay. I'm April. And I'm just thrilled as anything to be sitting here with you."

"Ah well."

The girl gazed at him as if not much time was left before he got back in the flying saucer. She said, "I've always had this big thing about wrestlers, the real pro boys, and even more with the famous ones."

Blasé: "I know how it is, April."

"Maybe it's every bit as absurd as my friends say, but who cares. I gave up fighting it long ago. I accept." She offered the book. "Could I have your autograph, please?"

When that had been flourishingly brought off, the name as legible as black skywriting at night, a waiter came. April asked for a dry martini. Apple asked for another of the same, which didn't give away that his drink was only ginger-ale.

Happily, proud of his quick thinking in containing the girl, Apple surreptitiously watched Stripper and the wrestler as they chatted, and gave attention to April while she talked about her job, high school teacher, and her absurd but gratifying predilection.

"Obsession, some might call it," she said at one stage. "But I don't worry about that. If there's one thing I can't resist it's a pro wrestler."

Looking at her with greater care, Apple saw that the girl was far more attractive than she at first had seemed. If she were to make the best of herself, instead of heading in the opposite direction, she would be quite outstanding, he mused, not missing a decided shapeliness under the prim clothing, a warmth in the eyes and the way she showed her bottom teeth—as though she shouldn't.

"It's nice to know I'm not a freak," April said when their drinks had been served. "Thousands of women feel the same. Maybe millions."

"You've always been this way?"

"For years and years."

"You have male pin-ups on your walls? Beefcake? You buy the wrestling magazines?"

"Oh no, nothing like that. No pics, no mags. I don't know a thing about the profession—rules and records and so on. I simply go for the men involved."

The last statement April repeated presently when their glasses were empty, at which time she was sitting beside Apple and had her hand on his thigh. He could no more recall how it had got there than he knew how his arm came to be around her shoulders.

She said, "I don't want to embarrass you, Bernie."

"You're not."

"But I can't help myself—especially when I've had a li'l drinkie."

In all honesty, Apple said, "I know what you mean."

"There're times, like now," April said, snuggling close and giving his thigh a squeeze, "when I'm just putty in a wrestler's hands."

After clearing his throat: "Oh?"

"That's nothing but the truth. Putty."

"Well now."

"Know what my ambition is, Bern?"

"No, April, I don't."

"My ambition is to be present when a professional wrestler is changing into his fighting gear. Just the two of us there. It's the ritual that sends me."

"Well, listen," Apple said.

How they actually arrived at the stage of leaving the lounge together, his motel the goal, he was unsure, but Apple did know he had paved the way by pointing out to himself that it was probably unethical for him to stay. One pro agent ought not to watch another at work, particularly if said work seemed to be running along splendidly, which it did.

They went outside with no dawdle to the rented car. Apple opened the passenger door first but then let April close it herself when he saw how unimpressed she was with the display of gallantry.

They drove off.

Sitting as close as she could without getting on his knee, the girl said, "I can't believe this is really happening."

"It is. Take my word."

"At last. A dream come true."

"Happy to oblige," Apple said as though he would rather be playing chess but was too noble a person to be able to refuse a lady a favour.

They turned into the motel.

Being the dead time of day, mid-afternoon, the time when all good reporters are drunk or napping or inventing copy, there was no one who represented a nuisance hanging around the Puck. Apple parked and led April up to his unit.

"Cute place, Bern," she said after looking around. She took off her spectacles.

"Thanks," Apple said, taking off his sunglasses.

The girl removed a back-comb from her hair. "Welcome."

"So are you," Apple said. "Here." He pulled off his yachting cap and tossed it aside.

April said, "How sweet." At the window she drew on strings to close the drapes, thus creating a reduced light.

"Sweet like you," Apple nearly said. He changed it to a tough, "Yeah."

Removing a bangle: "Right on, Bern."

Apple plucked off his false moustache. He stuck it on the wall and for a brief moment suffered real disappointment that there was no sort of portrait handy onto which he could have put the hairpiece, which would have been a terrific thing to do.

In the pleasant gloom April was heeling off her shoes. She said, "Might as well get comfy for the show."

"That's the way."

She stood barefoot near the end of the bed, facing Apple, who responded by taking off his own sneakers. He also took off his socks.

Her own ankle socks the girl shed stylishly, like pulling the skin off a serpent before it went into the stewpot. That done, she again faced Apple with hands on hips.

She said, "Okay."

He said, "Okay."

"Not feeling shy, are you, Bern?"

He was. "No."

Deafly: "Yes, I thought you were. All the big-name wrestlers are sensitive."

Densely: "No, I'm fine."

"Help you out," April said, getting hold of the hem of her sweater. She shuffled the garment up over her head and off, and flung it away with a grand-dame gesture as if she had been wanting to get rid of it for months. She wore an overburdened bra of frothy pink silk.

"There you go, Bern."

Apple made quick work of getting rid of the top part of his white track suit. In order to pretend he wasn't shy, he waited, pretending cunning.

"Oh, you sensitive toughies," the girl said fondly. She unzipped her skirt, let it fall, stepped free and footed it out of the way. Her pink briefs were so skimpy they looked frightened, ready to hide.

Absently awarding the lady ten points for the overall effect, Apple took off his trainer pants. He was relieved to see he was wearing plain shorts, not those he got last Christmas from an aunt, blue with little white elephants.

"Bern," April said, "I want you to know that this is a true treat for me."

"For me, too. You're gorgeous."

"But there's only one star here. You. Please continue."

Swaying: "Well . . ."

With another fond comment on sensitivity, April reached behind. She unfastened her bra. It leapt off, sailed forward and landed at Apple's feet. She quivered.

By stepping over the bra efficiently, Apple reckoned he had done his share in the ongoing tit-for-tat.

Evidently reckoning the same, April took hold of the sides of her briefs between pincered forefinger and thumb, plucked outward and started to shimmy the garment down, bending as she went.

Apple was so delighted that, once April was upright again, his hesitation about taking off his shorts lasted nowhere as long as it would have normally. It helped that by now he and the girl, with moving forward, were standing close.

One more step apiece and they were inches apart. Next, they were embracing.

Apple decided not to mention that this had little to do with the ritual of changing into wrestling dress. He caressed the girl's back, waist and hips, while she concentrated on kneading his shoulder muscles. He hoped she wouldn't divine that he was no real wrestler.

The telephone rang.

Apple said, "Oh no."

April whispered, "Answer it."

"Answer it?"

"Tell the desk you don't want to be disturbed again. I'll be able to rinse the taste of martini out of my mouth. Okay?"

"Neat thinking."

"Let's both be quick about it," April said as she retreated from his embrace. She went into the bathroom.

Apple took a deep, settling breath. He slouched like a successful womaniser as he went to the telephone at bedside and lifted its receiver. The caller was Chuck.

"I got news for you, One," he said. "Your plan doesn't seem to have worked out."

"How d'you know?"

"The gentleman in question has just been seen strolling along Emperor Avenue—alone."

Apple sighed around, "I'm not really surprised."

"What makes you say that?" agent Chuck asked. "Feeble plan to begin with?"

"Not at all, not at all. I was referring to the operative you sent. She certainly wouldn't have been *my* choice."

"I didn't know there was anything wrong with her."

"You must be kidding."

"Not at all. I vetted her personally."

"You were happy with the way she was decked out? That I find hard to believe."

Testily Chuck said, "Look, One, we know the gentleman and you don't, not even slightly. We know what type of female he goes for. I suppose you wanted something flashy."

"Well—"

"That operative we sent in is the same type as the gentleman's wife, and the same as all the girl-friends he had before he got married: subdued, no make-up, ordinary hair, a pair of eye-glasses, plain everyday clothes."

Apple stared into space.

After a pause Chuck asked, "You still there?"

"Yes."

"What's wrong?"

"Nothing. And you're quite right, Chuck. The girl was perfect. That's why I was kidding you—she couldn't've been perfecter. The deal didn't work out, that's all."

"Better luck with the next idea."

"By the by," Apple said. "What cover was the operative using?"

"April Jones, schoolteacher, true age, hobby—"

"Fine," Apple cut in as the bathroom door opened.

" 'Bye for now." He put the receiver down. The girl appeared and he told her, "Reporter from Montreal."

April said, standing there naked, "It's only natural that someone as famous as you is going to be pestered by the press."

That was his cue, Apple recognised drably. All he had to do now was say he was not the celebrated wrestler Bull Massive; which, in full fairness to himself, he had never actually claimed to be, only let it be assumed.

So he would confess, he thought, and they would laugh about it ruefully, the way colleagues do, and he would take the blame for the plan going awry, for presuming that Stripper was the operative when in all likelihood she was only a hooker. There was no difficulty.

Except, Apple mused as April came back into his arms and he felt her warm flesh as she kissed his neck, except that he would miss out on making love to this marvellous girl, which no real pro spook in his sane mind would miss out on. It was the fraud of a true bastard, and every red-blooded man had the right to be one of those at least once in his life.

Afterward, Apple thought, he would arrange to give the girl the straight story. He could do it indirectly, by saying he had to get ready for his bout tonight—Silver Flash versus Eskimo Mel.

April kissed that same neck spot again and ran a hand languidly down his spine, while he almost managed to span her waist with his hands. She, he supposed softly, was a faceless one.

What did it matter if she was?—Apple blustered, harsh. Who cared if the wench was out today on a rare mission? If this was her big opportunity to make good, be promoted? If she never got employed on a caper again, having picked up the wrong man? That was *her* problem.

For his own part, Apple wanted to know what it mattered if he was—yes, using the girl immorally and unethically. That's what your twenty-two-carat bastards did.

Thrilled in more ways than one, Apple murmured, "Let's try the bed, mmm?" His voice had the rake's drawl.

To avoid the stage door and its possible cluster of fans, Apple entered Empress Hall at the front. The house was full, the box-office closed, the ticket-taker absent, so he was able to pass straight through into the auditorium, where a wrestling bout was in full gasp. After circling behind the seating, he followed concrete passages to the changing room.

With the usual gathering of men present, Apple began to get into his silver garments. He had already had a shower at the motel with April, at which time he had at last been able to say his prepared piece to establish that he was not the glamorous Bull Massive.

The girl, whose back he had been soaping, turned to ask, "You're Eskimo Mel?"

"Silver Flash."

"Whomever, you're not the man I thought you were?"

"You've been thinking I was somebody else?"

"No no no," April had said in fluster, prelude to an involved explanation that she hadn't been following him too well. She ended brightly:

"But, of course, it doesn't really matter."

Now, with heat on his neck, and a blush which

shame was keeping down, Apple remembered that line, plus the girl's friendliness and her parting pat on the shoulder as though to say, "Don't worry about it, sonny."

Impotence, Apple told himself, that of the occasional variety, could happen to the best of men, as well as to bastards—even to real pro operatives, which is why he hadn't taken off his cover for the girl; she obviously hadn't been told, due to the need-to-know rule, that the wrestler called Silver Flash was a Brit agent.

She had taken the news of her caper's failure very well, Apple allowed after he bullied his shame aside. And he was glad that when he called Chuck, to tell him there would be no repeat, he explained that he had purposely kept April away from Bull Massive because of a startling new development in the mission.

This recollection of how smoothly he had arranged everything put Apple up several rungs, so that by the time he was ready, changed and in his cape, he was congratulating himself on his wiseness. He had preserved his strength for the coming bout.

Apple managed not to recognise that he was determined to lose the bout. He congratulated himself again.

Soon the wrestler from the previous match came in. He wore woe like a body stocking. He blamed failure, not uncommonly, on everything from the crowd's noise to his opponent's brand of aftershave.

Apple swept out.

As always in the auditorium, the entry of the gladiators and their introduction took up maximum time, to create maximum tension and interest, excitement and glamour.

The referee of this bout, a small dark man with a pointed face, was especially lavish in his introduction of Eskimo Mel, giving a long list of achievements.

The man in the corner opposite Apple could even have had enough Enuit blood to justify his name, though he looked mostly Oriental. His gimmick, apart from a robe made of furs, was mutton-chop whiskers that grew down to a meeting under his chin in the same shagginess as his hairline. He seemed to be wearing a fur-lined hood.

Apple didn't think much of the outfit, which struck him as crude when compared to his shimmering own. In any case, he was more interested in Agnes de Grace.

In her usual seat, parts of her wearing a purple dress, the blonde had been semi-distant with Apple. On his every circle of the ring to salute the crowd he had given her a private wave and smile, receiving in exchange a gracious but reserved nod, like that of a monarch whose ennui is seen as the imperiousness of the blood royal.

The actress's attitude, Apple felt, could have something to do with the fact that, intent on not looking at her upper legs, his gaze had tended to wander from her person altogether, which was hardly flattering.

Apple was on the verge of going to the ropes at that side to be more direct—without making mention of undergarments—when the bell rang. The bout was on.

The crowd gave voice, and the referee nimbled aside.

Leaping forward with a Yukon fell, Eskimo Mel landed in a tall squat, arms out, as if someone had just stolen his drink, cigarette and barstool.

Apple faced him in his own stance. It was one which, using a full-length mirror at home in Bloomsbury, he had refined from the pose taught him at Damian House. He had more curl to the fingers, less ugliness in the sneer, and his eyes were not so much wolfish as lionesque.

The two men circled.

"Make a splash, Flash!"

"Send him to hell, Mel!"

"Start a crash, Flash!"

"Do a hard sell, Mel!"

The crowd applauded each poet.

Wanting to appear willing, Apple rushed in. His opponent suddenly shot down into a ball, and Apple went straight over the top like leap-frog and into the ropes. They catapulted him back again. He fell over Eskimo Mel in reverse and landed clumsily on his head, which pealed with pain.

Next, Apple was lying flat to the canvas, pinned firmly by his opponent, who was grating, "Count, count."

The referee was crouched there beside them, his hand poised for pounding.

Eskimo Mel: "Count, you snail!"

The referee slapped canvas without enthusiasm. "One."

"Go *on,*" snarled the wrestler, who still had Apple's shoulders flat down, due partly to his strength and partly to Apple's connivance, though he did make a display of waving his legs.

"Well," the referee said, "two."

"Keep going," Eskimo Mel fumed. "You blind or something?"

The man probably did need glasses, Apple thought. To make things more obvious, he wriggled his shoulders, thus showing how totally pinned they were.

This wriggling, aided by the sweat of both parties, caused the pinning hands to slip off, which brought Eskimo Mel's head shooting down. His brow collided with Apple's nose, which filled his eyes instantly with tears. He squirmed out from under on account of he hated not being able to see what was going on.

Apple got to his feet. Eyes wiped clear of water, he saw Eskimo Mel getting up with a grim, true expression inside his ring of shaggy hair as he glanced back and forth between his opponent and the referee.

"Ring his bell, Mel!"

"Tie his sash, Flash!"

In hopes of making a good, bellicose impression, Apple flung himself at the other man, who, surprised, staggered back. If it hadn't been for the referee's presence behind him, he most likely would have kept his balance. As it was, Eskimo Mel fell over onto his back.

Automatically, Apple went across and pinned him. Almost before shoulders were touching canvas the referee was there and pounding with a fast, "One Two Three!"

The crowd roared approval and rage.

Apple got up in doubt, while Eskimo Mel lay on, gaping at space. Flashbulbs popped. The referee called out, "First fall to Silver Flash!"

Being bemused by the suddenness of events didn't prevent Apple from strutting around the ring in the acceptable fashion, like a cockerel circling the hen house to draw out custom. He flexed his muscles, smiled, winked.

When Apple got back around to the referee, the man was bellow-bandying words with Eskimo Mel, their matter unheard under the crowd's clamouring mixture of encouragement and disparagement. The poets were exchanging insults.

Apple, a lion who didn't care to be involved with the wolf pack, went on past for another strut.

During his second circuit of the ring he brought his eyes down from their Olympian level. This enabled him to see what he had missed before.

Agnes de Grace was no longer in her seat.

Apple stopped. He looked down at the vacancy. He was still wondering about it when the attack came.

It was from the side, a shoulder charge. Gladly, obligingly, Apple flung himself into a collapse, but had the bad luck to again land on his head, which gave a longer peal of hurt. He curled instinctively into a protective ball, which Eskimo Mel worked at unfurling, stooping and grappling and giving wet growls. When he succeeded, it was inadvertently; he touched a ticklish spot.

At that moment, Apple shrieked and slammed his legs out straight. His boots smashed at speed against the chest of Eskimo Mel, who flipped backward to sprawl out on his back like a four-pointed star.

The crowd racketed.

Apple got up. Then he got down again. But he saw that he couldn't avoid at least making a show. Crawling forward, he lay lightly across the other man's chest.

At once he heard from the referee a loud and rapid shout of, "One Two Three!"

Next Apple was standing amid the tumult, feeling dizzy from the bashes on his head, telling himself he was going to go straight home to bed. His arm was being held aloft by the referee, who was calling him cousin—a habit of North Americans that Apple liked.

FIVE

Next morning, Apple got up bright and fresh, no peals in his head. He felt even better after a shower because not once during it, he was fairly sure, had he thought of April. He was finishing getting into jeans and a sweater when the telephone cut into his unit's peace.

It was the desk. She said, "Gents of the press here to see Silver Flash."

Apple said, "I left word I wasn't to be disturbed."

"That was last night."

"Same word now."

"Too late," the girl said. "They're on their way up."

Apple broke records, he was sure, in slamming his bare feet into loafers, grabbing a large towel and going to the door. There he became as cautious as a sneak thief. Opening up a crack, peering out, he saw a group of men with Speedy Bane at their head. They were coming across centre court.

When they went from view beneath the outside walkway, Apple nipped out and sped along to the end, near the stairhead, where he was bending by the last unit's door, his back turned, towel over his head and shoulders, as the men came up onto the level. They hustled past.

Making the most of feeling triumphant over his trick, which was similar to the one he had used in escaping from Empress Hall last night, Apple went down the stairs lightly. Only after he was safely inside the Ford did he look back up at his unit, where the men were encouraging each other to knock harder, to rouse the sleeping wrestler.

Apple drove off whistling, with his eyebrows up as though he had just pulled off a major coup. He didn't settle to normal until, following a distance-making drive, he was opening a newspaper at a coffee-shop counter.

Fascinated, he read the lead story in the sports section. It was an account of his bout with Eskimo Mel, which sounded ten times longer and twenty times more exciting than the encounter he remembered. He read the story again.

Although annoyed with himself for allowing his natural aptitude for unarmed combat to emerge, and make him the winner, Apple was equally annoyed at the reporter's suggestion that the match might not have been won on skill alone; that, perhaps, the referee had been a shade hasty in his counting.

Suggestion became accusation in another article. It was an interview with the man who had lost. Eskimo Mel claimed that the count had been a jabber and that the referee must have been drunk or blind or half asleep or plain old-fashioned sick in the head, to put it politely.

Apple thought badly of poor losers all the way through his ham and eggs. Accepting a free second coffee, he asked the waitress, with a nod at the headline:

"Don't you hate excuses?"

"Sure do. My boy-friend says Eskimo Mel's a real nerd. A child could beat him. Wait'll the Flash meets Mammoth Morgan tonight. Oh boy."

"But Silver Flash is no pushover."

"Tell that to my boy-friend," the waitress said. In turning away she glanced out of the window and added, "There goes S.G."

After Apple had gone through every wrestler's name known to him, although without admitting to himself that he was doing this, he realised the waitress must have meant Samuel Glacier, who had been passing.

Apple paid and hurried out.

Seeing no signs of the professional gambler or his Rolls-Royce, Apple strolled along Emperor Avenue, his hands afted comfortably. He thought it a pity that he had to deliberately lose to Mammoth Morgan, and didn't even feel the slightest embarrassment at the thought.

At the dwindle of Emperor's downtown section, Apple turned and started back. When he halted it was because a voice hissed, "At your service."

Apple went to the lamp-post where Knotty leaned. He looked as if he were selling hot religious tracts. He said, "Hey there, kid. How's basketball?"

"Just fine, thanks."

"And what're we looking for today, huh?"

Craftily, Apple said, "A client of yours?"

"Now that's real interesting."

"Samuel Glacier by name."

"Ain't no client of mine, kid, believe me. The guy's so straight he can't sit down."

"So it appears, you mean."

"Naw, you get to know these things in my line of

trade," Knotty said. "He don't pop, shoot, snort or drop *anything.*"

Apple said, "What a shame."

"But if you want'm, he's over the way there in that snazzy-looking barber shop."

"Maybe getting into the hair tonic?"

"Kid, the guy hardly drinks. Like, straight."

After they had shaken heads at each other, Apple went on. He crossed the road to a position behind the parked cars, from where, at a distance and obliquely, he looked through the barber shop window.

He saw what he had failed to notice on passing the three-chair establishment earlier: one of the men waiting was Samuel Glacier, semi-obscured by the newspaper he was reading.

So far so splendid, Apple thought. The mark had been run to ground. Now all that was needed was a gimmick—something good and hot.

On the sidewalk but out of sight of the window, Apple began to pace. He fought for an idea. He strove for brilliance. He sought the perfect answer. But nothing came, either shiny or dull, hot or tepid.

Noting that he had paced too far that last time, Apple bustled back and then bent in the show of tying his shoelace—bent, not squatted. The extra flow of blood to his brain would help, he hoped.

It seemed to be working. Soon he came up with the notion of making a telephone call to the barber shop. The place being small, as well as poshly quiet, a strident voice on the phone would be heard by all.

Excellent, Apple thought proudly. So what would the voice have to say for itself when talking to Samuel Glacier?

It could be the gambler's poor old father, begging for money to pay the rent and buy a crust or two.

It could be a discarded mistress, crying for a crumb of kindness and understanding.

It could be a banker who was sorry to say he was unable to give Glacier any more loans.

It could be a bookmaker, either refusing credit or making threats in respect of money owed.

It could be a teenage girl, asking her despoiler what he was going to do about her pregnancy.

It could be an irate parent on whose children Glacier had set his brute of a dog.

Although impressed with his inventiveness, Apple was less impressed with the damaging potential of these slanders. He suspected that, far from creating odium, they might even lead eavesdroppers to look upon Samuel Glacier with admiration. In short, they weren't awful enough.

After a peek through the window (his mark was next in line for a chair), Apple went back to his act, pretending to work on the other shoelace.

He was at the point of admitting that he felt dizzy when a different approach came to him—the direct one. He would march into the sedate shop, and in a ringing tone charge Samuel Glacier with having . . . being . . . doing . . .

What?

Apple didn't know, though he did have a soft spot for the melodrama of the piece. Straightening, he wobbled slightly and then went back to pacing.

Minutes later, when an answer came, it was due to urgency. Danger had appeared in the shape of British wrestling fan John Bark, who still wore the baseball cap. He was striding this way.

At speed Apple mused that he would tell Samuel Glacier that he, Apple, was going to inform the police of this matter (not stated), unless Glacier immediately set about doing the legal and moral thing, with no whined excuses this time.

John Bark getting closer, Apple took a deep breath and strode over to the barber shop. He burst in and slammed the door closed behind him, stopped on the threshold and pointed at Samuel Glacier with a rigid arm.

Everyone had fallen silent. The three barbers stood with scissors and combs poised. Their chaired customers were watching via mirrors. The waiting clients, newspapers lowered, were eager for distraction.

Samuel Glacier's expression as he stared to see clearly, against the window's brightness, was half involved with the task of recognition.

Apple paused. This much localised attention he hadn't experienced in years. When sitting, impertinent height hidden, he never seemed to attract a first glance. At parties people sometimes leaned on him. Once a tipsy man had tried to stand a glass on his shoulder.

Feeling acute discomfort, Apple began to blush. The heat rushed up from his chest to his neck, and thence to his face, which became crimson. Worse, as always happened in such events, his mind went blank.

The silence creaked on, and everybody stared at the man standing with his arm out. Apple burned and suffered while trying to get his heated brain to work. He couldn't remember what he was doing here. He couldn't even recall his latest blush antidote.

As his gaze, unbidden, roved the upper walls in a stab at pretending there were no people present, Apple found his head clearing faintly. He remembered an old short-term cure. You had to imagine yourself as a missionary in a cannibal's stewpot. Being more silly than horrific, the cure had never been much good, and Apple doubted if it would help him now.

Nevertheless, he had almost decided to use the oldie, was letting his arm droop and starting to see that jungle glade, when the door behind him opened. Someone came in, drawing everyone's fast attention.

Tiredly, drearily, Apple waited for John Bark to speak. Instead he heard a different voice from the person at his back, a voice with all the lazy satisfaction and pseudo-boredom of a sensational newsbreaker.

The man said, "Well, I guess that changes things some."

Everybody, in unison: "What?"

"Oh, that old accident."

Half the assembly: "What old accident?"

"Why, the one that just happened. A four-car pile-up on the highway north of town."

A quarter: "Anyone hurt?"

"Naw, not seriously," the man said. "Lotsa broken bones and stuff. But six of the Festival rasslers were in it. Joy-riding, seems. This puts 'em outa the competition." He named names.

Everyone began to talk, granting Apple glances that seemed to say his odd behaviour was understood now; he had come in with the same news but, suffering stage fright or whatever, had been beaten out of his moment.

Samuel Glacier threw his newspaper aside, got up, and came to the threshold. He shot a frowned look up at Apple and went out in a hurry. He was followed by the newsbreaker, off in search of more custom.

"Changes things is right," one of the barbers said. "There's only two guys left. So tonight it'll be the final. Bull Massive versus Silver Flash."

Apple absorbed the news while walking back to the car. Then, driving, he became concerned not with wrestling, but with his mission. The Festival was rapidly coming to a close and he had accomplished a great deal of nothing in respect to the Trio. He was within reach of failure. As if that weren't bad enough, he hadn't even been able to keep a low profile.

Which would be more difficult than ever to do from here on, Apple mused nervously as, slowing to turn into the Puck Motel, he saw an enlarged group of reporters hanging about. Speeding up, he drove on past.

The press group would continue to grow, Apple realised. Not only was the previously unknown Silver Flash bigger news than ever, but another lodger at the Puck, co-finalist Bull Massive, was also of established fame. Next you knew, they would be bringing in the television cameras.

He would have to change his place of residence, Apple saw, if he was to have freedom of movement. Which meant he needed to draw the reporters away, so he could get in the motel to pack and check out. Then, unhindered, he could get to serious work on the caper and try to achieve at least one third of its objective.

Because he owned not the grain of a notion as to how he ought to go about this attempt at damaging in reputation one of the Trio, Apple cogitated at a fiendish pitch to produce a ruse for de-reportering the Puck long enough for him to act.

He drove slowly. With finger and thumb, he

pinched out his bottom lip. He cast his eyes about for clues, his memory about for bits of usable business from books and films. He wondered if he should make a quick stop at a coffee shop for toast with lemon marmalade, which he believed to be the most efficacious brain food.

Apple smiled. An idea had appeared. Credit for it he generously gave, since he was fond of a hint of the mystical, to his having merely cast a thought toward his favourite snack.

Making a U-turn, he headed back along Emperor with an eye out for John Bark. He was sure that if he could talk the English fan into impersonating him, vaguely, by driving in and immediately out of the motel frontage, the copy scavengers would surely have to follow.

Apple assured himself that he wasn't overly distressed when, following two slow trips along the main street, he still hadn't seen the tall, pale, pimply fan with his awful buck teeth and those spectacles. But he admitted that he didn't have the beginnings of an answer to the question of how he could get John Bark to do the impersonation.

His next idea on de-reportering threw its hat in the door as Apple was again approaching his motel. He slowed still more, thought about it, pulled in the side and parked.

The corner telephone Apple walked back to was of the cowl kind. Boosted by this gift, he dialled and spoke in confidence. He told the Puck's desk to inform the fourth estaters that Silver Flash was giving a press conference at once in Ben's Beanery, out on the highway east.

One minute and twenty seconds later, by Apple's

watch, cars came surging out of the motel. Last gone, Apple ducked from under the cowl, ran to his car and slammed inside. He sped on to the Puck, where he stopped quickly, darted in the office to ask for his bill to be prepared, raced to the stairs, and went up and into his unit.

He started throwing items into bags.

The telephone rang.

Apple snatched up the receiver, growling. He was less annoyed with the interruption than with his moronic inability to leave a ringing telephone unanswered.

The caller was the Festival's bout coordinator. Importantly he said, "It is my duty to apprise you of—"

"I know," Apple snapped. "So long."

"Wait wait."

"What?"

Voice flat: "You know? You've heard? About the accident?"

"Yes. See you."

"Wait," the coordinator said. "You know about Crusher Tulip's broken arm, John the Beef's dislocated wrist, Long Leonardo's badly fractured . . ."

"Yes," Apple snapped. "And the others. All six are out and I'm in. With Bull Massive. Adios."

"Wait. There's no afternoon show, of course. Your match goes on at nine, after two prelims by amateurs."

"So good-bye."

"We're arranging a conference for TV and press at the hall afterwards," the coordinator said. "That's all for now. I have to go. So much to do. Good-bye." The line died.

With another growl, Apple flung the receiver down. It missed the cradle. After two seconds wasted in retrieving it—growl turned to whine at his madness—he returned to his bags.

There sounded a screech of car brakes.

They couldn't be back already, Apple assured himself as he darted to the window. Below, rocking from its fast halt, was a stretch limousine.

Its driver's door opened. Out stepped Agnes de Grace. She wore tight pants and a punished sweater. Ignoring the motel office, she made straight toward the stairs.

If she was coming here—and she could hardly be going anywhere else—fine. Apple thought this without considering the neatness of the blonde's arrival.

He went back to his battle of packing. He stuffed a shirt into one bag and closed it; a pair of socks he tossed toward the other bag and perked when they went in.

As footfalls from outside stopped at the door, Apple darted there and snatched it open. The actress had her hand raised for knocking. She smiled, swayed, changed to a salute.

"Anybody home?" she asked perkily.

"Only just," Apple said, turning away. "I'm delighted to see you, but I can't ask you to stay because I'm not staying myself."

"What's wrong?"

"I'll explain while I get on with this."

"And why did you stand me up the other night?"

Packing busily: "I stand you up? No, I was there out front. The limo wasn't."

"I was in a different car," Agnes de Grace said. "But we'll sort that out later. What's all this about?"

After telling of the four-car accident, irked to find the job enjoyable, Apple said, "I'm being besieged by reporters and fans. I have to leave here as of five minutes ago."

"Where you going?"

"No idea."

"The town's full to the nostrils."

"Don't I know it."

"Well, look," the blonde said, "come to my place, at least for the time being."

"Aggers, that's a great suggestion and I accept," Apple said. "I'll follow you out there."

"No, darling, I'll wait for you."

"Even better."

"Let me help you pack."

Minutes later, bill settled, Apple was steering out onto Emperor Avenue behind the limousine and telling himself that, now that he had been smart enough to get this far, he wasn't going to biblical-sense the situation up. From here on it was the mission and nothing but the mission. Sentiment must not be allowed to interfere, and the carnal even less.

They stopped side by side in front of the house, whose tenant was out and up the steps first. She was opening the door with a key when Apple joined her.

She said, "My maid and the houseman're having a day off, which is nice of me."

"Ah," Apple said slowly and significantly, although, he told himself, his deliberate measure was because the lady most probably expected something along those lines; the tone was to remind agent One to forget significance.

They went inside, into a hall and then through an arch, into a large living room. Its furnishings were Thirties Modern, except for the bar, which was Space

Travel. It was a plastic entity that travelled with her everywhere, in sections, Agnes de Grace explained as she went behind it, where she looked exceptionally at home.

Dipso Actress Carts Own Bar Around, Apple tried as a tabloid headline, which he found interesting until he heard, "Too bad I'm not much of a drinker."

He gave another, "Ah."

"But I do like to entertain, and as this is a special occasion maybe we could open a bottle of champers. What do you think, darling?"

"I don't care for champagne," Apple said, playing it cool. "Why is this a special occasion?"

Agnes de Grace looked around with, "Um."

"You mean because I'm wrestling in the final tonight with Bull Massive?"

"That's right. I mean—what? You're in the final? You ought to have told me. But I think you did. There's so much going on, isn't there, darling?"

"True, Aggers."

"Anyway, my congratulations. How wonderful. But that means we have to forget champers."

"I don't like it."

"I hate to say no to anyone but I don't think you should have any alcohol. You're in training."

"I know," Apple said. "In any case, the drink I like most is sherry on the rocks."

Agnes de Grace waggled a hand like a metronome. "Sorry, darling. No booze today."

"I agree."

"No arguments."

"Okay."

"However, there's nothing wrong with coffee."

"Except the caffeine," Apple said. "No, thanks."

"That's right. The same goes for tea. How d'you feel about hot chocolate?"

Because his hostess was trying so hard to please, Apple said, "Love it."

"Hold the fort with cannon," the blonde said as she came out from behind the bar. "Hot chocolate coming up." She went out with a ratatat of high heels and a cavorting of hips.

Apple took the place she had just vacated. With hands flat on the bar, arms stiff and shoulders hunched, he asked space, "What'll it be?"

Sighing, he got a glimmer of understanding in relation to the bar-owner's tyranny. And knowing that power wasn't good for you, he left the bar, whereupon he noticed a writing desk.

Shrewd move, One, he thought as he went to it. He carefully, unsqueakily, pulled down the flap. The pigeonholes held a poor collection of papers (the actress was here only temporarily, he reminded himself).

Apple drew out a letter, then opened and read it. It was a note of thanks from a charitable protection-of-wildlife society, for Ms. de Grace's generous contribution.

His mouth in a downturned crescent, Apple exchanged the letter for another. This one, from a kennel, said that Fifita, Ms. de Grace's pet poodle of great age, was doing as well as could be expected in her mommy's absence.

Apple shuddered. That didn't prevent him from remembering that he still hadn't got around to sending a postcard to his Ibizan hound, Monico.

The third letter Apple read was from a Calgary orphanage. Its principal expressed her gratitude for the signed photographs the children had received from Ms. de Grace.

Apple was relieved when footfalls clicking in the distance made him put back letter four unread. He returned the writing desk to order and loped to the bar, where he sat on one of the fronting stools.

The blonde came in with two cups. With a broad smile, Apple fought his hesitant disappointment on seeing that she was still wearing her clothes.

"Ah, chocolate," he said.

"Made with the real melted McCoy instead of powder. I don't do this for everybody, darling."

"I'm flattered."

"I'm flattered as well," Agnes de Grace said, "having here a finalist for the championship." She put down her cups and slid one to Apple. "There now."

He took a sip. "Delicious."

"Good. So you drink that all up like a clever boy while I go make a phone call or two." She left again.

Apple looked at his cup. With regret, he realised that to finish the chocolate would be a mistake. The vast amount of sugar would do him no good whatever. Bravely, he got up and crossed to one of the various potted plants and poured the drink into its soil. He was long back at the bar, humming, when Agnes de Grace returned. She took the next stool.

After giving him a piercing glance she said, "Darling, you look tense."

"I do?"

"Absolutely. I hope you're feeling all right."

"You understand what it's like, being hounded by fans and reporters," Apple said. He realised he should have known his guilt would let him down, even when he wasn't aware he had any. "It's pretty harrowing."

"Maybe what you need is a good hot shower."

"That, Aggers, is a terrific idea." He reminded himself that he got some of his best, most convoluted schemes while showering or lounging in a bath.

"Then please be my guest."

"The only thing is, being in a shower alone in a strange place makes me nervous."

Smiling languidly, Agnes de Grace said, "You don't have to be alone, darling." Getting off her stool, she held out a hand. "Come with Aggers."

They left the room, crossed the hall to a broad staircase and went to the upper floor. A door near the stairhead led to a master bedroom, off which was a bathroom of sumptuous but unflashy appointments.

After she turned the water on in the shower stall, the hostess said, "Last one to get undressed is a fried egg."

Working quickly—due both to eagerness, and to the fact that speed prevented him from having to admit he would never be able to say smart things like that—Apple got out of his clothes. The strip was a draw.

Agnes de Grace swooshed into the stall. "Come on, lover."

Apple joined her. His head and shoulders being above the jet of water didn't bother him. He could see all the better. He could see his companion's back when he soaped it; he could see over her shoulders as, reaching both hands around, he gave a more thorough soaping to her breasts.

Apple was beginning to wander farther afield when the blonde said, "This, I gather, isn't doing your tension any good."

"We can't have everything."

"A massage, that's what you need."

"Go ahead."

"Not here, lying down."

"Aggers, you're full of brilliant ideas," Apple said, not caring about his own emptiness of the same.

"Switch the water off, darling."

They left the shower stall and helped each other get dry. At one point Apple paused at a sound from outdoors. He asked, "What was that?"

"What?"

"Sounded like a car."

"Yes," the actress said. "Mailman."

Dry, they went into the other room, where Apple, as instructed, stretched himself out on the star-size bed, on his front. When she was kneeling beside him, Agnes de Grace took a bottle of baby oil from the bedside table and annointed his spine. Spreading the drool, she started to massage his shoulders.

Apple lifted his head. "Listen."

"To what, darling?"

"It sounded like another car."

"Yes, darling. It's the baker."

"You get good service here."

"Close your eyes," the actress said in a soothing tone. "Just relax." She went on with her gentle stroking. "Let yourself drift like a feather."

Apple felt easy and drowsy. It was a pleasure to let his eyelids sink. The hands on his back made his muscles, overworked this week, purr like spoiled kittens.

So peaceful and spoiled did Apple feel that when, presently, he heard Agnes de Grace ask him softly if he were asleep, he didn't answer at once. Then, before he could, she answered for him.

She said, "Of course you are."

Not wishing to disabuse his masseuse of her conviction that her labours had been a total success, Apple said nothing, though he did give a satisfied mumble.

Agnes de Grace got quietly off the bed. Opening one eye a fraction, casually interested, Apple saw her put a robe on over her nudity, step into slippers, and leave the room. He raised up to listen. As he had expected—knowing how some people were about their mail—he heard footfalls go downstairs.

The next thing Apple heard was voices. Since letters and loaves were incapable of speech, he leapt off the bed.

The mumble he heard floating up from below, Apple knew by the tone, was one of those social exchanges that are never listened to by the people who make them, just as nobody ever honestly answers the question, "How do you do?"

Apple was on the verge of turning away from his place at the stairhead—peering down into the empty hall, thinking a neighbour had dropped in—when the situation took a fast turn.

Apple realised that in addition to Agnes de Grace's voice, there were two that belonged to males, that he had heard them before, and that they were known to him. The men were Bull Massive and Samuel Glacier.

Apple gaped around him like a child in Wonderland. Instinct told him that this was no innocent meeting for a hand or two of cards. The Trio seemed to be a trio.

Agnes de Grace said, "Glad you guys helped yourselves to drinks and all."

Samuel Glacier said, "Sure."

Bull Massive rumbled, "We know the ropes."

Their voices were faint, coming from the living room beyond the arch. Apple knew he would have to go closer. But he didn't want to risk missing a single word by getting his clothes or even some sort of cover. So he began to creep down toward the hall as he was, naked.

Agnes de Grace said, "I couldn't join you sooner. He has the constitution of a horse."

Bull Massive: "No sweat."

Samuel Glacier: "There's no hurry, Agnes."

"I expected him to be out like a light when I went back from calling you guys. Those sleeping pills're really strong. I loaded his hot chocolate."

"Did he drink it all?" Glacier asked.

"He loved the stuff," the actress said. "Anyway, then I expected him to pass out in the shower. But no. Lively as a cricket. But when I got him on the bed he finally drifted off. A horse, I tell you."

"You just ain't any good at the Mickey Finn routine, honey," Bull Massive said, a grin in his voice.

"Huh, look who's talking."

"What's 'at mean?"

"That dope you gave Silver Flash in the champers wasn't so great. It was supposed to make him *lose,* y'know."

"We've been through this before."

Samuel Glacier said, "Now now, kiddies. Let's not squabble. There were bound to be mistakes and setbacks in a project as complex as this one."

"Yeah, right," the wrestler said. "And congrats, Aggers. You didn't waste any time locating the guy and you did bring him here."

"Yes, Agnes, fast work."

"Thanks, fellas. I was all shook up, as the song goes. I nearly dropped dead when you called about the accident."

Glacier: "I should have had it in all contracts that they weren't supposed to travel together."

"They shoulda known better," Bull Massive said.

Agnes de Grace: "I'll drink to that. Who's dry?"

To a background of convivial inconsequentials, Apple crept on down to the bottom of the stairs. He tiptoed over to one side of the arch, unaware that his hands were fanned in front of his groin.

Getting down on hands and knees, Apple lowered his head until it was at foot-level, as he had been taught to do in Training Seven. Not only was it the last place people's eyes would go to if they suspected a pryer, it had the best chance of being covered—by a piece of furniture or other objects.

Apple moved his head forward cautiously, until he could see to his right into the large room. He had a clear view of the bar. On its stools sat the two visitors; their hostess stood behind. All three looked pleased.

After a sip of his tonic water, Samuel Glacier said, "Yes, Silver Flash will be safe here until bout-time. We don't want any more accidents."

Bull Massive said, "No, and neither do we want him beaten up or crippled by someone. Meaning three or four wrestlers that are sort of looking for him."

"And don't forget the reporters," Agnes de Grace said. "As if they haven't enough on their tiny minds with the pile-up. Wasn't that something?"

"As it happens," the gambler said, "it isn't going to hurt us. We know who's going to win tonight and bets are going on accordingly. Which is the reason for this meeting." He tapped a blue ledger that lay before him on the bar. "I'll bring you up to date."

Raising his glass of milk, the wrestler said, "I can listen to money talk any old time."

Apple felt the same over the following minutes. It was with grim elation that he began to see the whole picture. It was created by what Samuel Glacier had to say, plus the questions and comments of the other two, plus reminiscences and reflections, plus connecting facts already known to Apple.

The gambler, the wrestler and the actress were long-term buddies, siblings under the skin. They had met for the first time in a doorway. Each had run into it to hide from the riot-police, who were indiscriminately attacking anyone in sight, in their drive to break up a demonstration in support of Sid Street, the anarchist.

The police attitude had changed the Trio from mere observers into sympathisers, while their mutual celebrity changed them in time from strangers to friends, since each suffered in some degree from the loneliness brought by fame.

It was after they had known one another for some years that they hatched a plan whereby they would make a great deal of money. Each was in need of cash. Agnes de Grace, tired of being offered bit-parts—if offered any parts at all—had invested heavily in a self-starring movie that was so bad it had never been released. Samuel Glacier had gone to Europe to show those Old Worlders a thing or two and had sustained crippling losses in the casinos. Bull Massive was just plain greedy.

The plan started with organizing a wrestling festival to find, in quotes, a world champion. It ended with the Trio betting on the winner, without it being a gamble.

Everything would be fixed. Sex and sympathy and narcotics would be used on wrestlers and referees to ensure victory for the one on whom the Trio had placed their bets, which would be spread across the whole of North America. To obtain the longest odds, they would select an outsider.

Things had gone awry when their chosen boy, Mad Mountain Phil, failed to beat Silver Flash, even though the latter had been primed for defeat with a dash of dope from Bull Massive, and promises of sexual favours from Agnes de Grace—coupled with sad tales of her supposed cousin's physical frailties and career desires. The unknown Silver Flash had become the new outsider choice, and then he won another bout against Eskimo Mel, through an arrangement with the referee. Bets were down, through middlemen.

Reading his ledger, Samuel Glacier quoted the different odds he was getting from various cities. In his smug expression could be read, "No one would suspect a big-time gambler of promoting a competition in order to gamble on its outcome; it was far too obvious a move."

He looked up. "Those prices suit?"

"They're beautiful, Sam," the wrestler said happily. He had been strolling about the room, hands pocketed, with stops to sniff at potted flora. "We're gonna clean up."

"Like ten new brushes," Agnes de Grace said. "And that's not all. Like, I've been thinking."

Both men: "Yes?"

"With the Festival turning out sweetly for us, why don't we make it an annual event?"

The three started to discuss the proposal with enthusiasm. Apple wondered if the time had come for him to withdraw; it was the danger as well as the fact that his neck was aching and his bottom was cold.

The discussion having run its course, decision left

for some other time, Samuel Glacier closed his ledger. He said, "There's one other matter."

"Wait a bit," the wrestler said.

"Yes?"

"Aggers, what's the name of this one?"

Apple tensed. Even before he stuck his head out farther in order to see Bull Massive, who had wandered out of his scan, he knew he would be at the hot chocolate's burial pot.

The actress said, "No idea, honey. It's Japanese, I guess. Most of 'em are."

"Smells real funny."

"That right?"

"Kinda sweet."

"Like money, you mean?"

With a cozy laugh Bull Massive turned away from the plant pot. "Go ahead, Sam."

Apple relaxed and did a turtle. He hoped his bent legs weren't going to fall asleep.

Samuel Glacier was saying, "There's a wild outside chance that someone's on to us. Or maybe just on to me. It's a possibility that has to be considered."

Frowning, Agnes de Grace asked, "How do you mean? Some kind of investigator?"

"I don't know. But for several days now a guy's been shadowing me, getting under my feet. Or at any rate, that's my impression. You two had anything like that?"

They said a lingering, "No."

Bull Massive added, "I've had those nuisance calls I told you about. I don't see a connexion. I'm always getting them."

The gambler said, "He's tall, this guy, and has a red face. That strike a bell?"

Agnes de Grace shook her head and the wrestler said, "Not much of a description, Sam."

"I know, but he's got one of those real ordinary, uninteresting faces, the kind you see millions of."

The way Apple breathed in through his nose was so loud he had to stop midway for fear of being heard. He thrust out his jaw instead. But his delight that the Trio had turned out to be baddies was enhanced.

Bull Massive asked, "Should we worry about it?"

"No," the gambler said. "However, I'm not taking any chances with this guy. He could be a harmless nut but I'm bringing down a couple of heavies from Toronto. They'll remove him smoothly from the scene."

"That's the stuff, darling. Anything else?"

"Not a thing."

Bull Massive stretched himself luxuriously around. "Guess we'll head back to town, Sam."

Swiftly Apple withdrew, got up, went to the staircase. As he started climbing he heard Agnes de Grace say, "Take care of that ledger, darling. It's dynamite."

Samuel Glacier answered, "It's going where no one'll think of looking for it."

Apple's first moment of panic came when, back in the master bedroom, he couldn't see his clothes. Remembering where he had undressed, he dashed into the bathroom and swiftly reversed that process. His next panic came when he couldn't find a window that would open.

Apple was scared enough to admit to being so. He was aware that if the Trio knew or even suspected that their plot had been uncovered, he would be put out of action, perhaps permanently—the fate that awaited the tall shadower whose blush at least had been a fair disguise.

Apple tip-toed out onto the landing, and edged cautiously to the stairhead. Below, Agnes de Grace was at the front door, saying good-bye to her guests.

Softly Apple went along the landing to a window. He lifted the latch, and it opened without a sound. But then he stopped. It had occurred to him that, if he left covertly this way, it would be assumed immediately that he had eavesdropped.

Apple crept back to the bedroom. "See you later," Agnes de Grace was calling as he reached it. Feverishly, he started to look around for writing material. He had his ears creakingly alert for sounds of approach, even though he knew they would be muffled by his movements.

On a vanity table he found paper and an eyebrow pencil. The note, scribbled while listening to two cars start up and drive off, was to the effect that he had been awakened by the singing of a rare Speckled Bandicoot, which he was going to follow, if he could get the window open.

Apple left the note on his pillow, glanced at the vanity table in regret (why hadn't he had the nerve to write in lipstick on the mirror, something he'd always wanted to do?), and went to the door. Scene clean, he ran to the landing window, which he left blatantly open after he had climbed through, and saw that he would not, as expected, have to risk injuring himself with a drop: a drainpipe was handy.

Getting into position, Apple descended in textbook fashion. That it actually worked—and to perfection—so surprised him that he took his time. Finally he was standing on the ground, at which point he found himself looking obliquely into a kitchen window an armreach away.

Looking out of the window at him was Agnes de Grace. She gave a slow blink.

There followed a pause, with both parties blank of face, before Apple went into action. He did a fast mime. With prayer hands beside his face he acted sleep; springing open glared eyes, he performed coming awake fast; a hand behind his ear meant listening; by pointing aloft and flapping his arms he did a bird; that it was an important bird he conveyed by putting invisible binoculars to his eyes; he acted hasty writing; he made chasing motions.

Calm and inscrutable, Agnes de Grace opened the window. She asked, "What?"

"Read the note on the bed," Apple gabbled. He looked up. "There she goes!" He ran off.

"Come back," the actress snapped. "You need sleep."

Apple went on, staying beside the wall. He rounded the house and got to his car. Rumpling inside, he got the motor started and drove away. He did so with his eyes cast upward through the windshield in case Agnes de Grace had come to the front and was watching.

When he had straightened out in order not to hit a tree, Apple sped on toward the gate. He was hoping the gambler's Rolls-Royce convertible would still be in sight. The mission would be successfully over if he could get his hands on that blue ledger.

He turned onto the highway. All that could be seen ahead, in the direction of town, was a broad, lumbering truck. He quickly caught up, passed it and raced on toward the next car, beyond which he spotted the Rolls-Royce.

Not until he was drawing close to the car in front did Apple notice the driver's shiny, hairless head. It was Bull Massive. Apple dropped back.

Fuming, he had to stay there. He daren't risk being seen. Whistling raucously helped his frustration a shade, as did knocking his knees together and reminding himself of how well he had done in getting to the bottom of the Festival conspiracy.

Other cars passed; the Rolls-Royce drew steadily ahead and then got blocked from sight; Bull Massive continued driving at a circumspect pace.

Just when Apple was deciding to take a chance, and pass the car in front with his head turned away, it was too late. They were coming into busier traffic, close to downtown Empire.

Soon Bull Massive swung off. Spurting on, Apple switched his gaze about in search of the luxury convertible. It wasn't to be seen. He reduced to a crawl and examined every parking lot and side turning.

Coming at last to the dwindle of Emperor Avenue, Apple circled, started back. He still saw nothing. Direct action was called for, he concluded, so he steered into a quiet side street and parked.

The first person Apple saw as he strode around the corner onto the main street, intending to find a public telephone, was John Bark, the English wrestling fan. Apple couldn't escape. They almost collided.

Grabbing an arm, Bark said, "There you are at last."

"Mistaken identity," Apple said, trying to pull free, glad the other man looked awful in the baseball cap.

"No such thing. I believe I know who you are. And if I do, I don't know you."

"I never was any good at conundrums."

"No tricks, now. I haven't forgotten that thing with this." He touched the cap.

"Wear it in good health. It's you."

"You nearly got me into trouble with the police."

Apple said, "Discuss it with the British Ambassador. He's in that car over there." As John Bark looked around, Apple jerked his arm loose and stalked to the nearest shop. Its window was full of cakes and pastries.

Inside, after snicking the lock, Apple circled the counter while telling a staff pair and several customers breezily, "It's nothing to worry about, folks."

Everyone began to look worried.

"Be all over in two shakes of a lamb's tail," Apple said. "He's not all that dangerous." One good thing about being tall, he reflected with thanks, was that people were willing to accept you as a policeman on a mere hint of same.

John Bark was knocking on the door, and earning everyone's worried attention, as Apple passed through a rear doorway. He hurried past clutter and a pale man in white, whom he told, "I imagine so." Opening an exterior door, he went out into a yard, and from there gained an alley.

At its end, he turned away from the main street and marched to an unambitious grocery store. The telephone was occupied. He stood nearby, humming and snapping his fingers and tapping one foot, until the caller came haughtily out of the booth.

Apple slipped in. Within seconds he was talking to the bout coordinator, who asked, "What statement?"

"The one made by Mr. Glacier saying he didn't like it where he was staying, at the Grand."

"He isn't staying at the Grand. Are you resting up for your match tonight?"

"I'm sprawled out here on the bed," Apple said. "I'll be there on the dot."

"Good. This whole thing was nearly a disaster."

"Are you sure Mr. Glacier isn't at the Grand?"

"Positive."

"That's what I told these people. I said he was at the Ritz and quite happy."

"You're wrong, S.F.," the coordinator said. "Happy he may be but there's no hotel in Empire called the Ritz."

"How about that."

"Mr. Glacier is at the Dominion."

Grinning, Apple said, "Then it must be his room number that's in question. Gamblers are, I know, superstitious. But if he doesn't like 352 he could always change."

"The town's crammed tight. And I don't understand this foolish talk anyway. I don't know the number of Mr. Glacier's room, but I'm sure it wouldn't bother him in the slightest, whatever it was."

"See you later," Apple said. He disconnected, half satisfied. Yet he was also only half satisfied in respect of the hotel room being the right place. The man's lodgings didn't seem to be a place where no one would think of looking for the ledger.

Apple scanned about cautiously before leaving the grocery store. With his shoulders raised—this served no purpose but he seemed incapable of not doing it—he walked two quiet blocks, went onto Emperor Avenue and crossed over to the large, dignified Dominion.

Inside, he dropped his shoulders as he wended to the reception desk, where he saw he would have to wait for attention. He turned to look around the lobby.

At the same time, two men were turning from a showcase of costume jewellery. They saw Apple. Apple saw them. After they had exchanged a glance with each other, Tiny Bomb and Eskimo Mel began to come over.

Leaving the desk, Apple went at his special walk into the lobby's loiterers. He headed for the door. The way he twisted and turned without bumping anyone filled him with admiration for his skill.

Door reached safely, Apple went outside and stalked off at a brisk pace along the sidewalk. He threw a glance behind. The two wrestlers were coming. Furthermore, they looked happy, which meant they had something satisfying in mind, Apple knew, just as he knew that the something would not be to his own satisfaction, to put it mildly.

On the corner ahead stood a uniformed policeman. Apple went straight to him and said, "Excuse me, officer."

"Yes, sir?"

Apple pointed back the way he had come. "That hotel." He appeared to be pointing at the wrestlers. It was a never-fail trick.

The officer said, "It's the Dominion."

"That's right. I was wondering how old it is."

Tiny Bomb and Eskimo Mel had stopped. They swayed, coughed into their fists, shambled over to the curb, pretended interest in the passing traffic.

The policeman was so long in answering the query that Apple looked at him, whereupon he saw he was being stared at. Next, he recognised the man as the motor-cycle cop whose motor-cycle he had borrowed.

"Thank you," Apple said.

The officer said, "Hold on a sec."

"Oh God, I left the toaster on."

"What?"

Apple ran.

At the next corner, he turned off Emperor Avenue. That he didn't bump into someone who was after him for some reason or another came as a vague disappointment; it would have been so satisfyingly outrageous.

Shouts from behind fainter, Apple charged on to the mouth of a service lane. Again he was glad of his height, appreciative of the long legs that made him a good runner.

The lane, choked with delivery trucks, was a dead-end, Apple saw after he had entered. With almost no hesitation, he climbed onto a lowered tailgate, ignoring the box-laden interior which might have attracted an untrained mind. He grabbed the metal framework above and pulled himself up. He was lying flat on the canvas roof by the time he heard sounds of search from below.

Apple listened with a faint smile, cozy in body from the sun, cozy in mind from the feeling of persecution and the fed paranoia. He closed his eyes.

When he awoke, Apple was annoyed with himself for having fallen asleep; it was so appropriate of nothing. Besides, he was chilly, the sun no longer touching where he lay. But his post-slumber grumpiness soon left, as he treated body and limbs to a good rubbing.

After sensing his surroundings for danger, and peering in all directions, Apple climbed down to the ground. His belly growled a complaint. Of the several things he needed, he agreed, food should come first.

Cautious investigation of the back doors of businesses showed them to be wanting. Apple left the lane and went straight across the street into another. Here he found a perfection that would have made him feel depressed if he hadn't had so much else to contend with.

Beyond the department store's rear entrance there were service stairs. Apple ascended to the top-floor cafeteria, which he checked for enemies before entering. Following a leisurely satisfying of Need One with a hamburger and a salad, he went down to the basement, again using the service stairs.

"*Your* size, sir?" asked the girl in charge of the counter called Men's Underwear. She was smiling with one side of her mouth. "What size do you take?"

"I have no idea," Apple admitted. "I never bought long-johns before."

"Who bought them for you?"

"Nobody. Never wore 'em."

"Well, that's the largest size, at the end."

Shifting along the counter, Apple picked up an off-white garment that reminded him unpleasantly of the corpse of a decapitated ghost. Holding it against himself, he darted a warning glare at the girl, who looked away with eyebrows raised like a bored queen.

Sizewise, it would just about suffice, Apple reckoned. He asked, "Do you have it in any other colour?" He had had a vivid warrior-red in mind, or perhaps a safari khaki.

"Afraid not, sir," the girl said. "But what you could do is, you could dye it."

"No time for that," Apple told her absently.

"Not that it matters. I mean, who's going to see you in your underwear?"

"Only everybody. Wrap it up, please."

Bravely, Apple took the escalator up to the first floor. At the counter called Stationery, he bought newspaper-size sheets of heavy white cardboard, a ball of string and a black crayon.

Prudently going out onto Emperor Avenue with his purchases held up near his face, Apple assured himself of the necessity of the unglamorous long-johns. He needed to keep warm, and he needed to appear slapdash and non-legitimate.

After making his way in darts and lingers to the rented Ford, Apple drove out of town. It took some time to find what he wanted—a deserted spot. Where there were no houses or traffic there were joggers, cyclists, farmers and lost tourists. Finally he found solitude behind a farmhouse which bore a For Sale sign.

There he stripped and put on the long underwear. It was short in the sleeve and leg, generous of body, loose of neckline, sending that someday biography far back into the dimmest recess of Apple's mind.

Getting out spare Silver Flash gear, he donned trunks and boots, hood and cape—all with ease except for the trunks, which had to be wrestled with and sworn at before he could get them to fit over the nether bulk of the long-johns. With ease he was able to resist examining his reflection in the car window.

The sandwich-board Apple made by hinging the pieces of cardboard together with string. On each side he crayoned, TONIGHT! SILVER FLASH MEETS BULL MASSIVE! He was unaware that the second name was slightly smaller, and fainter, than the first.

Apple drove back into town. He parked, then

walked away from the car with his board in place, message broadcast fore and aft. He told himself he looked fine, just fine.

Within metres he earned a response. Children in a front yard stopped their play to stare, to point, to shriek with glee. Apple went on, his head rocking to show how little he cared.

There was more attention out on Emperor, though not so disrespectful. Passersby paused or moved aside or ventured a spurt of applause. Apple was glad of his mask.

Two of the pausers were Mad Mountain Phil and Batter Brown, strolling together. They stood to watch the sandwich man go by, and told each other what they would like to do to that pukey Flash, and *would* do if they got half a chance.

Thrilled by the success of his trick of dressing up as his own imitator, Apple went on to the Dominion Hotel. The stir he caused in the lobby won him fast service from a reception clerk, whom he told:

"I have to leave a message under Mr. Glacier's door."

"Leave it here."

"It's official and private, so I'll have to traipse up to the room personally, worst luck. Number, please."

He got it. Looking over at the block of pigeonholes, he saw dangling from that number's box a key-tab; the room was at present vacant.

Glancing around sternly for smilers, Apple went to a lift. He got taken up by an operator who confided that he believed Silver Flash was a member of the British Royal Family.

The corridor leading to Samuel Glacier's room was empty. Apple, who hadn't forgotten to bring his penknife, used one of its tools to get the door unlocked. He went in. His search lasted thirty minutes. It should have lasted five, but he so enjoyed what he so rarely got the chance to do, that he worked with great diligence and care, making sure everything looked the way he had found it.

There was no ledger.

Apple went down the stairs, which allowed him to make a better entrance into the lobby, since he was beginning to feel that he might not look so bad after all. He stalked grandly across and out. He held to his manner even when a police car passed slowly and its occupants gave him a searching stare.

He went to the barber shop. Inside, all talk and movement halted completely during the one minute he spent peering onto shelves, into cupboards and under chairs. Then he left, closing the door quietly behind him.

Continuing along Emperor Avenue, some of the tang went out of Apple's stalk when three small boys started to follow him. They jeered and blew raspberries. Hissing at them to go away served only to make them louder. They were quickly joined by a drunk and a camera-clad tourist. People ahead stood in wait for the parade.

As Apple was busily thinking about escape routes, he saw the Rolls-Royce convertible. It passed at a crawl. In the front were its owner and his dog, in the back a pair of men who had to be the Toronto heavies—men with flat noses to clash with expensive suits. They and Samuel Glacier looked solemnly at the walking advertisement.

When the Rolls had gone by, Apple moved into the roadway, where he flagged down a taxi. He got in.

Until they drove on, he was photographed by the tourist, jeered by the boys, waved at by the drunk. He got taken to the pool hall.

First, cleverly, he went to the refreshment counter. Its keeper he told, "I came to collect the book Mr. Glacier left here with you. The blue one."

The man said, "Ain't nobody left no books here. What am I, a library?"

"It's a ledger."

"I'm a bank?"

It had still been a clever idea, Apple thought as he went to a table at the back. He interrupted play long enough to search around—fruitlessly, but not without creating a certain amount of awe.

Descending to Emperor, Apple got in the waiting taxi. He asked the driver to take him to the tavern where he had watched the gambler play cards. There, after trying his clever idea on the bartender, he did a search. The whole was watched with fascination by all present, one of whom, a drunk, went around telling people, "I seen'm. I seen'm already."

Apple had the cabbie drop him centrally on the main street, being unsure where exactly he had left the Ford. He walked on with caution. He was wary of enemies and terrified of small boys.

A man coming out of a cafe ordered, "Stop." Short and plump, he wore an overcoat with a velvet collar.

Halting, Apple looked at him as he would at a stranger. "You mean me?"

Harshly, the coordinator asked, "Who hired you?"

In a Viennese accent Apple said, "It my own idea to help glorious wrestle game."

"Was it Silver Flash himself?"

"No no."

"Bull Massive?"

Seeing a patrol car approaching at a cruise, Apple was forced to end the enjoyable exchange. "I promise Mr. Bull I no say nothing," he said, sweeping on.

Over the following minutes, Apple saw Agnes de Grace, reporter Speedy Bane and Eskimo Mel, one after the other in separate cars, each driving slowly and looking around. He lurked along until he caught sight, in an off-street, of the Rolls-Royce, which he decided was what he had been seeking.

He walked toward the car. Getting the dog away from the car should be child's play, he mused in recalling bits of business from Training Nine. An attitude of authority was all you needed.

Apple came to a stop beside the convertible, right by where its guard sat. He said a firm, "You."

Looking up at him, the dog silently showed its teeth.

Of a sudden, Apple realised that Samuel Glacier's own car was hardly a place no one would think of looking. He backed off and turned. He saw the two Toronto heavies. They were standing watching him. He turned again and ran.

SIX

He had seen the movie before. Twice. The first time had been in a London cinema, the second was on the plane coming over. He hadn't cared for it on that first occasion, and the plane screening he had watched only to help in ignoring his constricted legs and claustrophobia. Now he wished he had something to help him ignore the movie.

What he really hated—Apple explained to himself in order to lighten his burden by seeming less small-minded—was not the motion picture itself, with its sickly leading man and fatuous plot, but the fact of having to stay here.

He had to sit still. He had to hide until bout time. When everything had been going at full tilt, suddenly it had all come to a halt. The excitement was on hold.

After the treat of a good, heavy sigh, Apple once more tried to give his attention to the film. The six-foot-tall, good-looking hero with dark wavy hair and a confident smile was too awful. Apple sought diversion in dwelling on a screenplay of his own.

It was about how he had escaped from the pair of heavies. He shuffled happily in seeing an idealised version of his ingenious doublings and twistings through streets and alleys—on one of which he had discarded the sandwich-board—and his final bold dash across Emperor to the movie house. He left off-screen the reality of the two heavies having ended their chase puffingly at the second corner.

Left out also, when Apple returned to his burden, was the reminder that all action had halted and the excitement was on hold because there were no reasons for them to thrive, at the moment. He had nowhere else to search for the blue ledger.

But he knew that the mission-clincher had to be somewhere close. It was in a place with which he was familiar, and he felt certain that the answer would come to him before this evening was finished.

If not—if he didn't find the ledger himself—Apple acknowledged morosely that he would then do the correct thing, and report its existence to contact man Chuck. He and his department would move in, take over, and do the finding with ease. The mission would be brought to a successful close. But agent One would not have personally done the closing. He would not have won with a flourish.

Apple sneered at the screen.

One and a half hours later, with the common-sense part of his mind on the time, Apple got up. He had to go. He started to do so, his eyes not leaving the screen's images. Shuffling slowly, he went along the row, dawdling up the aisle in reverse.

It wasn't anything to do with the heroine being much prettier than he recalled, Apple would have defended if he had needed to. It was nothing to do with her plight being much more harrowing. It was simply that he couldn't believe a leading man could be that bad.

His fists clenched because he knew, as he wrenched himself away, that the girl was going to make the wrong decision about that stupid letter. Apple went out into a corridor. By the time he had left the building via an emergency door, exchanging brightness for the tar-black of an alley, he had come to terms with knowing it was only a movie.

The dark turned to gloom as Apple became accustomed to the night, which was a chill one, winter saying that Indian summer had been around long enough. He had to fight reluctance to remove his trunks and boots, then strip off the warm long-johns. He shivered violently, but knew that part of it was due to feeling a return of the excitement.

Silver accessories on again, cape snugly around him, Apple went to the alley's end, where it met Emperor. The stage ahead was set, he knew. Before going to a seat in the movie house, he had telephoned in a message for the Festival bout-coordinator: for personal reasons relating to meditation, Silver Flash would be changing elsewhere and would make his appearance when he was announced from the ring.

The main street, though brightly lit, was quiet. Apple slipped out. Not wondering about what a finder of the abandoned long-johns would think, he loped along to Empress Hall. Its ticket office was dark; its doors were locked.

But even as Apple stared through the glass into the lobby, tingling at the thought of everything going terribly wrong, an usher appeared, stopped, stared back. He came to the door and drew it open wide.

"Come in, Mr. Flash."

"Thank you," Apple said, entering. "Please inform the master of ceremonies that all is well."

"Yes, sir. And the best of luck."

"Guess I'll need it."

"Well, Bull Massive's only the best, that's all."

Which, Apple mused, was why the odds were long on the dark horse, who had to be allowed to win for the syndicate of three to clean up.

He went into the auditorium. It was dim apart from the bright cone of light over the ring, where the last of the exhibition matches was in progress.

Finding a place to stand behind the seating, Apple mused further on the subject that if by some fluke Bull Massive won the final bout, he and his two partners would lose their roll. Which would be nice, a poetic justice. So why shouldn't they lose *and* be disgraced?

Apple mulled this over, uninterrupted by a flurry of indifferent applause from the crowd. Also he considered the idea of getting his opponent into a secret service hold and threatening to disable him permanently unless he gave away the ledger's whereabouts. But Apple doubted if the wrestler would be privy to Samuel Glacier's doings.

In addition to that, he doubted his own ability to make the hold work right, in which case Bull Massive might turn nasty and do some permanent disabling himself.

This thought took Apple's attention to the ring. The two amateurs were wrestling with so much skill, so little acting and flamboyance, that they would never be able to make the step down to the money-earning ranks. Had Apple realised that his smile was patronising, not appreciative, he would have been more hurt than embarrassed.

A hand touched his back.

Nervously he whirled. He twitched loose again on

seeing the youth, who was leaning back from the whirl, his ballpoint and autograph book raised like weapons of defence.

Relaxing also, the youth asked, "Would you sign for me, please, Mr. Flash?"

Apple would. After handing the booklet back he said, "If this were full of famous signatures, worth a fortune, and you wanted it to be safe, where would you hide it?"

"In a bank."

Which Apple didn't want to hear. But as he turned away, the youth leaving, he reminded himself that he still had the bout to play with, if not the caper's final chapter.

A lethargic quality in the atmosphere dissolved: the exhibition match had ended. People stirred, roused, talked at a more animated level. The auditorium's full lighting coming on, Apple was able to pick out certain faces.

In her usual seat at ringside, flanked by adoring matrons, was Agnes de Grace. She wore a skimpy dress in hysterical yellow. Her expression was unreadable.

On the far side of the ring from the actress sat Samuel Glacier, inscrutable also. Behind him sat one of the Toronto heavies, with the other farther back in an aisle seat.

Scattered around in the front rows were Tiny Bomb, Batter Brown, Eskimo Mel and Mad Mountain Phil. Not one of them looked particularly happy.

At the nearest aisle's top stood several reporters, among them Speedy Bane, while on other aisles were policemen with familiar faces and wrestling fan John Bark.

Lights dimmed again. The main bout was about to start.

The master of ceremonies entered the ring, patting his tuxedo as though it needed reassurance. His yammer into the lowered microphone was followed by a tape of trumpets, which was joined by cheering as Bull Massive and entourage came down an aisle with pomp and flourish.

The next yammer was still going on when Apple left his place and strode ringward, to more cheers. He raised both arms because he couldn't help it.

The master of ceremonies left the ring after shaking hands with his replacement, the referee, who shook the combatants' hands as they climbed through the ropes. Silver Flash and Bull Massive delighted the crowd by merely exchanging cool nods before going to their respective corners.

"Don't be so dull, Bull!"

"You're just trash, Flash!"

After removing his cape and settling his hood, Apple strolled to the place at the ropes above where Agnes de Grace sat. She smiled and waved. Her expression was readable as contented. Her panties were seeable as yellow.

"Where've you been?" she mouthed.

"Here and there," Apple said in the same fashion, but more elaborately.

"What happened with the bird?"

"Caught it."

"Clever you," Agnes de Grace said.

"But it's illegal to keep them, so I don't know where I can hide it."

"Why not try a plain old bird-cage?"

"Ah," Apple mouthed. He was still thinking about that suggestion, offspring of Edgar Allen Poe's *Purloined Letter,* when he was called by the referee.

At ring's centre the combatants stood face to face, suitably sullen, while the white-dressed third man went through his rapid spiel about no eye-gouging, nostril-poking, ear-biting, rabbit-punching, crotch-kicking, mouth-heeling, throat-crushing or finger-bending.

"Is all that clear?" he asked, darting looks up from man to man.

In the time-honoured tradition of the professional game, both wrestlers nodded deeply while saying, "No."

The referee waved them to back off, signalled to ringside and stepped aside as the bell rang for the bout to start.

The wrestlers circled each other, the crowd roared its encouragement. Most shouters seemed to be for the national favourite, Bull Massive, but many were for the unknown and unorthodox outsider. Some were for neither, but against either; this anti-ism was the reason for their presence.

"Make him null, Bull!"

"Ya got no pull, Bull!"

"Start to bash, Flash!"

"You're no better'n a rash, Flash!"

His features contorted with venom, Bull Massive rushed forward. If Apple had taken what he saw as true, he would have been afraid. As it was, startled by the other man's portrayal of hate and ferocity, he did nothing to avoid the rush and was knocked down.

Instead of falling on top of his floored opponent, which was what a segment of the crowd was screamingly advising, the bald wrestler grabbed an arm. He pulled. It appeared as though he were trying to tug the limb off; in reality, he was pulling his adversary upright.

It was well done, Apple had to admit when he gained his feet. With a weak flail, he got his arm free. Again he and Bull Massive went into their circling. They feinted and snorted and grimaced and stamped.

Stepping in, Apple tossed an indifferent judo chop. Not only was it slack, it was aimed for a foot away from the neck of Bull Massive, who, however, brilliantly moved himself into line. He thus managed to get the feeble blow to land.

Bull Massive staggered back. His face was advertising pain and dismay, his legs were doing rubber. After bouncing off the ropes, he twirled brokenly. That finished, he fell to the canvas, where he lay on his back, arms spread.

"Pin'm, Flash!"

Apple responded to this multi-voice screech by turning toward the crowd with a hand cupped behind his ear, as though to ask, "What was that?"

The advice was repeated with greater volume from even more throats, while other voices were ranting at Bull Massive to get up before it was too late. He raised his head a fraction, the better to see what was happening.

Many ringsiders were on their feet, including Agnes de Grace and Samuel Glacier. Shaking her fists, the actress yelled, "Get him, get him!" The gambler merely stared.

From part of the crowd came a questioning mumble.

Bull Massive jumped up. His expression a cross between the genuine bemused and the phony fierce, he came predatoring after Apple, who backed away. He kept on with his reversing despite orders from the crowd, the referee and Massive himself to stand his ground and fight.

Agnes de Grace yelled, "Kill the bum!" She and other people were still on their feet in order to shout or see.

Bull Massive made a charge, arms out. Apple dodged aside. He also dodged the next two similar charges. On the fourth he stood still. The out-thrust arms he grabbed at the same time as he let himself fall down backward. His opponent was obliged to stumblingly follow.

Apple finished up with his shoulders on the canvas and with Bull Massive's hands clamped on those shoulders, which the bald wrestler was unable to stop doing because his elbow-nerves were being pressed by Apple, at whom he stared down in the anguish of a bad winner.

The referee came, crouched, checked that both shoulders were in contact with the canvas, pounded it three times to match his count, got up calling, "First fall to Bull Massive!"

The crowd's racket was composed of jubilation from the rabid Massive fans, hoots of indignation from Silver Flash supporters, semi-derisive moans from the neutral lovers of free-style wrestling, and from those who were against both wrestlers loud jeers for the winner.

The combatants got up. Apple pretended to look dejected but still defiant. Bull Massive stood in a sag, looking shocked. Agnes de Grace, sinking back into her seat, looked worried. Samuel Glacier looked angry.

The referee waved the wrestlers toward one another. Apple went forward. He did so as though he were having to force himself to do it, to be brave.

Brave of him it was, Apple thought, to be putting on the chicken bit. After all, he had to consider his legion of loyal fans, who were advising him noisily to have dash, be brash and pash, make a clash.

Bull Massive started to back off. This caused such a storm of protest and mockery that, after only two or three steps, he stopped. With Apple keeping up his forward trek, something had to happen. It did. It was the bald man giving a yell and grabbing Apple around the waist. He hoisted him high and sideways, then flung him down.

But it was professionally done, appearing five times worse than it was, and the vicious-looking kick that Massive sent into the descending body formed, in reality, a helping brake.

Apple, lying on his side, was about to roll over onto his back, be available for pinning in case his opponent forgot about losing, when Bull Massive rolled him the other way. He sat on him, straddling amidships. He began to fiddle with the zip fastener at the nape of his hood.

Apple understood at once. The other man was going to take the hood off, this to both explain why he was keeping Silver Flash on his front, safely unpinnable, and to make it appear as though he were pulling out all stops in order to win, even employing psychology: remove a person's mask and you damage his confidence, since we're all braver with our faces hidden.

Bull Massive got the fastener open. Pulling the hood off, which Apple was unable to prevent, he waved it over his head as he got up to do a dance of triumph.

It was a good piece of theatre, loved by everyone as

far as that part of it went, although there were murmurs of disappointment about the revealed face—a disappointment which Apple naturally took to be not in connexion with the array of features, but that they didn't belong to somebody famous.

These complaints, however, Apple noted as he got to his feet, came not from those who found the revelation of particular, personal interest—namely Speedy Bane, the pair of Toronto heavies, the British wrestling fan, assorted policemen and, especially, Samuel Glacier.

The crowd was yelling for more. It wanted action, it wanted blood to flow, it wanted to bear witness to pain. Above all, it wanted Silver Flash to retaliate for being belittled. The yells swooped up when he seemed to be obliging, when he crept toward his still-prancing adversary.

A faint smile of relief flicked across Bull Massive's mouth as he saw Apple's approach from the corner of his vision. He gave another smile of light gratitude as—pretending to be taken by surprise, therefore unresistant—his arm was fiercely grabbed; another smile of respect when he obviously recognised as unusual the grip that was taken on wrist and bicep.

Tossing the silver hood aside, Bull Massive swept into a beautiful performance of mortal agony, hand clutched to brow, head thrown back, one foot tapping canvas.

The crowd was ecstatic.

Now, Apple thought, when he had stopped looking at the grins of Agnes de Grace and the gambler. Now. Which was the most important, to extract the location of the ledger or to make Bull Massive win? The answer, of course, was that if the hiding place was a mystery to the wrestler, which was quite probable, word would be flashed to Samuel Glacier that the ledger's existence was known about—and it would vanish from wherever it was into the nearest fire.

But could that be the way to do the finding?—Apple queried. Let Massive give the office to Glacier, who naturally would waste no time about going directly to the ledger in order to bring about its destruction, with agent One not a thousand miles behind, ready to grab the evidence?

And what if Silver Flash couldn't get away from the ring fast enough?—Apple countered. And that managed, what if he failed at keeping a close, covert tail on Samuel Glacier to wherever it was he was hastening?

With glitter, Apple wondered: Is *that* where the blue ledger might be?

Not wishing to spend any more time on the match, Apple closed with his opponent. He made sure their arms were a tangle, so it wouldn't be clear who was the aggressor. Putting on a face of agony of his own, he began to sink toward the canvas. He drew Bull Massive down with him, and got a perverse pleasure out of seeing the phony expression change to one of consternation, as the message got through that the grip would have to be obeyed.

"Be a bull, Bull!"

"Lots of flash, Flash!"

"You're an empty hull, Bull!"

"You're just trash, Flash!"

Declining to acknowledge that it was only through the other man's passive cooperation that he had been able to take up this arcane espionage hold in the first place, Apple went on drawing Bull Massive with him as he sank, slowly.

He finished up on his back and with the wrestler lying across his chest. Massive started gasping oaths and contorting his features and straining muscles in an attempt to escape from this winning position.

Apple got his shoulders flat, the referee was there to pound out his count of three—and the bout was over. Bull Massive was the champion.

The crowd went wild.

Hold released, Apple rolled out from beneath his hapless conqueror, leaving him to flounder, and jumped up in sprightly fashion. After accepting a sympathetic handshake from the referee, he circled, bowing crowdward, his manner one of regret.

Everybody was standing, some on their seats. Samuel Glacier was hidden from view, but Agnes de Grace was right there in front and she looked stricken, staring up, ajar of mouth.

Apple was aware of derision in the crowd's noise, of sardonic boos, of suggestions that the fix was in, which he was happy about; but he was also aware that every second counted, that he had to be elsewhere while, conveniently, everyone was here. Nor did he forget that he was a wanted man.

Detouring Bull Massive, who was sitting up with head in hands, Apple slipped through the ropes. He grabbed his silver cape from the ring's apron as he jumped down.

The first of the several people in the aisle was a Toronto heavy, whose hands were raised in containment. Apple feinted one way, dodged the other, got around the broken-nosed man and went on.

As he darted up the aisle, zagging, Apple was touched by many hands. Some contacts were pats of condolence, some jabs of disgust, some attempts at grabbing. He was too concerned with escape to sort one from another, in respect of the attendant face.

Following a final skirmish with a policeman at the aisle's top, Apple reached the lobby. He dashed to the doors. Next he was outside and bursting off into a run, one in which he intended to hit top speed and which would end only when he arrived at his car.

At a babble of commotion Apple glanced back. Several people had appeared under the Empress Hall marquee. Prominent among them were Speedy Bane, one of the heavies, the motor-cycle cop and Samuel Glacier, who had the blank face of fury. As they gave chase, others came out behind them.

Apple ran in confidence. He felt sure he could outrun any of his pursuers, so long as they stayed on foot. Even so, on noticing a taxicab cruising in the same direction, across the avenue, he took the opportunity to lessen risk further.

As he ran into the roadway, Apple looked behind again. Now there seemed to be fifteen or twenty men strung out along the sidewalk. It made Apple feel decidedly uneasy and enormously flattered.

In answer to a shout, the taxi came to a stop. Reaching it, Apple squeezed into the back and panted out a direction. He added:

"Quick. I'm escaping from reporters."

The driver, fat and swarthy, turned to look the other way, to where the posse was charging diagonally across the road, fan John Bark leading by a head over Eskimo Mel. Snapping back to his wheel, the driver zoomed off.

He asked, "You that guy I heard about that's been advertising the rassling?"

"That's right."

"So what they want with you, them people?"

Apple said, "They think I'm the real Silver Flash."

"I got two dollars on'm to win."

"He just lost."

The driver said, "Next time I'll stick to the ponies."

Putting his cape around him and fastening the neck-clasp, Apple promised himself that when he came to pay for this ride, which might not happen tonight, depending on what developed, he would add two dollars to a decent tip.

This made him feel so good, his legs stopped shivering at the cold. He covered them affectionately with his cape.

The thousands of people who would be financially damaged by his defeat, when he could easily have won, Apple had put off dwelling on until later. At the moment he was being strictly professional; the pro accepts that in the spy game it's usually the innocent who get hurt—rarely the players.

Having left Emperor Avenue behind, the taxi was cutting through residential blocks, changing direction at every corner. It came onto another broad thoroughfare and continued heading out of town, speed on the build.

Apple looked back. The road was deserted under its high lighting. Then, just as he was turning away, into view rushed several cars, which, like his taxi, were breaking the speed laws. As he turned to face front, a police-car siren started to yip.

"Faster," he said. "I'll double your fare."

"Cops after you?"

"I didn't have a licence to be a sandwich man, among other bits and pieces."

Gunning his motor, the driver said happily, "Okay, if you back me up when I tell 'em you forced me."

"My pleasure."

"With a gun."

"I don't have a gun," Apple said. Absently he added another truth: "I don't like guns."

"You got a knife?"

"A teensy-weensy thing."

"A knife is a knife," the cabbie said. "Anyway, I didn't see the size, only felt the point. You held it to my neck."

Apple rested his forearms on the seat in front. "Right," he said. "Let's go."

"Yes, sir. I'm no hero."

They sped on into the quiet, dwindling suburb. Ahead were traffic lights at a junction. The light was on red but the cross-roads were deserted. Humming, the driver went straight through. Ahead now was dark countryside.

Looking back with a blasé smile, Apple saw all the pursuing vehicles crash the junction also. One of the cars, lying at the rear and trying to pass, had on its top a flashing light. The siren yipped on.

The police car still hadn't got to the head of the fast motorcade when, within minutes, the taxi was swinging through a gateway in a white fence.

"Sure," the cabbie said. "This is the place rented by that blond actress, right?"

"Right. Agnes de Grace."

"Boy, is she a looker."

"You ought to see her undressed," Apple wished he could say. He said, "I agree."

The gateway was being entered by the lead chase

car as the cabbie brought his taxi to a screechy halt in front of the house steps.

"Stick around," Apple said, getting out.

"Guess I'll have to."

Apple bounded up to the front door. Not unexpectedly, it was locked. He ran along the porch, grabbed a wicker chair and smashed it feet first into the nearest window.

Cars were stopping and their doors were being opened as Apple finished battering the window-frame free of shards. He stepped inside. He thought all he needed now was to have got himself into a locked room.

He went to the door. It was open. He passed through. Beyond was dimly lighted.

Along a passage, via a kitchen, Apple came into the large living room. Enjoying the sound of pursuit from behind and of fists bashing the front door, he went straight to the writing desk.

He pulled down the flap. Lying there openly was the blue ledger. He snatched it up. After sparing one second to look inside to verify, he moved on and raced through the arch.

He almost bumped into a uniformed policeman, who fell back against Speedy Bane, who bumped into a pair of reporters, who sprawled against a Toronto heavy. By then, Apple was midway up the stairs, chased by shouts.

Hitting the landing, he raced to the end window. He shot it open, and, ledger in teeth piratesquely, went out onto the drain-pipe. Swiftly, he descended.

"There he goes!" called someone at ground level as Apple ran onto a lawn. Other shouts from above and below were thrown after him as he charged ahead. But he knew he had got free.

Even while hearing the music of victory, however, even while thrilling to the moment's magic, Apple, recognising that the scene would never be believed in all its melodrama, was composing a suitable paragraph:

Shrewdly, agent Porter had thought to grab up a grey blanket before he leapt from the window. With this wrapped hidingly over his silver garments, he was able to slip away into the dark, unseen —a shadow who made no noise other than a soft chuckle.

A touch of martyr in his smile, Apple ran blithely on, the cape floating out behind him.

ABOUT THE AUTHOR

Marc Lovell is the author of thirteen previous Appleton Porter novels, including *The Spy Who Fell off the Back of a Bus* and *That Great Big Trenchcoat in the Sky. Apple Spy in the Sky* was made into the film *Trouble with Spies.* Mr. Lovell has lived for nearly thirty years on the island of Majorca.